There You Are

There You Are

A Romancing the Doctors Romance

Ieshia Wiedlin

TULE
PUBLISHING

There You Are

Dedication

FOR DADDY

Acknowledgements

It takes a lot of work, and a lot of time to write a story. To put your ideas on a page of imaginary people who have lived in your head for months and months. To make them real, loveable, and fun. Many people have played a role in bringing the lives in this story to life, and I would like to thank them all.

I want to thank my mom Linda, who introduced me into the world of reading. Multiple trips to the library growing up, and of course introducing me to romance novels with her stash of Danielle Steele books. Thank you mom for all of your encouragement, when I felt like all of this seemed silly. You reminded me of how much I loved writing and telling stories even when I was a kid. Love you mom.

I want to thank my husband Brian, and my kids Lucas and Zoey. For months and months you guys endured mommy sitting with her face glued to her laptop, and headphones blasting music in my ears. I appreciate your patience, your understanding, and for bringing me snacks and coffee. Most importantly, I thank you for loving me, and pushing me to keep writing when I felt hopeless. I love you all very much.

I want to thank my brothers Dell and Herman for providing me with all the laughter I needed to keep me going. All the texts, and jokes they provided to keep my spirit fed and uplifted when I felt like I didn't have what it took to keep on going. You guys always sent just the right message, at just the right time to refocus my mind.

I want to thank Wendy, Sarah, and Marla for reading all of my early drafts. For providing honest critiques that only your best girlfriends can provide. I want to thank you for your truth, and your willingness to take the time from your busy lives to help me. I appreciate you ladies.

I want to thank the Tule Publishing team for taking a chance on me, and believing in this story to share with the world. And I want to thank my editor Julie Sturgeon for dealing with my anxiety over my mistakes and errors, and all the many emails I sent her way. She, along with the rest of Tule, kept believing in me.

Lastly, I want to thank my father Herman Sr. I want to thank you for telling me I could do anything. I know when I first told you I was writing a book you told me how proud you were of me, and that I could do it. Well Daddy I did it! I want to thank you for always believing in me, no matter what. Knowing how proud you were of me kept me going, and I hope that I will continue to make you proud. I hoped you would've been here when this came out, but I know you are smiling overjoyed for me. There's no way this happened without you pushing me to have faith, truth, love, and joy my entire life. I love you forever daddy.

Readers, I hope that you feel all of the love, joy and happiness in this story. That it brings a smile to your face, and it's a story that you can enjoy time and time again. I thank you and appreciate you giving it a chance.

Ieshia

Chapter One

A MINA WRIGHT STOOD in front of the window in her hotel room. She stared at the lake and watched the waves lap against the shoreline. She needed every bit of calm the lake view brought to her to steady her nerves for the charity gala she'd organized. This event was held every year, and the Chicago Bulls were counting on her to turn out another success. Amina had reached out for speakers this year and needed a higher number of donations. The needs in the community had been much higher the last few years.

She'd decided on a black off-the-shoulder dress fitted to hug her curves in all the right places. She put on one of her indie playlists to soothe her mood, and she tried to figure out whether or not she wanted her locs all up or down and decided a cute updo would work. Sure, she would have to endure hours of Spanx and high heels, but it would be worth it. She swayed in front of the mirror while she applied her makeup when a knock at the door pulled her from her thoughts.

Angela Miles stood in the doorway. She looked stunning

in a red, fitted strapless dress. Her caramel skin glowed, and her long hair framed her striking face. She was ready to set the room on fire.

Angela hugged Amina tight and stood back to check her out. "Hey, lady, are you ready to go?"

"Yes, girl!" Amina smoothed out her dress across her belly. "Just trying to make sure no one asks me if I'm pregnant!"

Angela made a face. "What is this music you're playing right now?"

"Hey, don't hate on the Real Estate." Amina turned the music up as guitar licks filled the room.

"I feel like I need to take a nap right now. You should be in here getting hyped up!"

"This is my hype music!" With a grin, Amina danced to the smooth beat.

"How our friendship has survived this long, I'll never know."

Amina had known Angela since tenth grade. Amina helped her pass their biology class with her endless obsessive notes, and provided her the best advice she could ever get. Even though she didn't always follow it. Angela was her oldest, dearest friend, and if anyone understood Amina, it was Angela.

"Oh, you love me." Amina laughed.

"Anyway, Mina, you look beautiful. So glad you went with the black dress over the red one. Less skanky."

"Yes, because there can only be one skank in the room."

"Hey, I am what I am." Angela playfully hit Amina in the arm. "I'm so happy this event is here. It's been months since I've been able to get out of the house to do anything without David."

David, Angela's eleven-year-old son, worked so hard helping around the house to make things easy for his mom, but even so, Angela had to have a break, and Amina loved to give it to her. For the last four years, Angela had lived for this night so she could cut loose, perhaps meet a handsome guy, and be downright reckless. She had lived up to the reckless part for sure. Amina wasn't sure how the guy last year made it out of her hotel room.

Angela elbowed her friend. "Any plans on bringing anyone back to this room tonight?"

"Um, yeah, no." Amina adjusted herself in her dress. "I just want to go to this gala, have a few drinks, shake some hands, thank some doctors, and come back here in time for *Sportscenter*."

"Girl, you need to get out there. There's no reason for you not to be dating. All this hotness is going to waste. I know, it's been tough for you to trust anyone after Omar, but you have to be willing."

Amina slid into her shoes. Her friend meant well.

"I have moved on, Angie. I'm open to the possibility, but I just haven't met anyone worth the time. What's the point if you know it's not going anywhere?"

"Well, if something happens tonight, just go with it.

Maybe it doesn't need to lead to anything, you know? Just don't overthink. That room is crawling with fine men, and doctors too."

"Yes, I know, Angie. I've met a lot of them before."

She shrugged. "I'm just saying. It's been more than two years, and you are a beautiful woman. If it happens, go with it, okay?"

Amina slowly nodded as they walked out the door of her hotel room.

Chapter Two

"I HATE GOING to this shit." Dr. Nathan Moore exhaled and fixed his bow tie in the mirror of his bedroom. He knew it was essential to attend these events for the hospital, but he never enjoyed it. He was on his second shot of whiskey and prayed that it took the edge off his frayed and aggravated nerves.

His best friend, Shawn, had convinced him earlier in the week to attend the gala. "Women love doctors, and you need to get some action. This event is the perfect place." Shawn's tall build and coffee skin was catnip for women in any room, and he soaked it all up. He was clearly hoping Nathan would get just as lucky.

"Shawn, how desperate do you think I am?"

"I just want to see you happy. That's all, bro."

"And you think having sex with random women, on the strength of I'm a doctor, is key to that happiness?"

"Why, of course!"

Nathan shook his head as he remembered his conversation with Shawn, who was downstairs grooving in his loft.

Nathan shrugged and tried to get his head ready for the night. Women, drinks, music shouldn't be too bad. A few final checks, another shot of whiskey, and both men were out the door.

Nathan and Shawn arrived at the Field Museum for the charity gala. They walked the red carpet that extended from the sidewalk, up the stairs, to the main hall, and through the museum to Maximo, the dinosaur, as it waited for guests to arrive. When Nathan came into the main hall, his gaze darted around the room in search of the bar. He heard the acoustic guitar of a small band playing off the entranceway, and the scent of pink and red roses filled his nose. Tables and small couches were spread throughout the main hall, with a stage just in front of this massive dinosaur. Too bad the dinosaur had to spend the night surrounded by all the pink and red flowers. Hopefully, one year he would walk into something like this a bit less over-the-top, and much less like his high school prom.

"Ladies, the best-looking doctors of the night have arrived," Shawn said as he and Nathan laughed.

Shawn winked and waved at women on the way to the bar, where he and Nathan opened up a tab. They worked the room as they shook hands and he spoke with a variety of different women who leaned into him, reached for his hand. Forcing a smile on in his face, he bought them a drink or two, but he wasn't interested.

If this was what the night would bring his way, he was

ready to leave. As they talked about hospital politics with a group of young doctors, Nathan plotted his exit.

And then the sight of a beautiful woman on the stage freed him from those thoughts.

"Good evening. Thank you, everyone, for coming tonight as we celebrate all of the contributions to the Robert Lurie Children's Hospital."

Her brown skin glowed, and he wanted to reach out and touch every inch of it. Her shoulder was perfect as it peeked out from her dress and taunted him. Nathan stood and stroked his beard as he imagined how flawless the rest of her would be.

"Please, everyone, take some time to meet each other, have a drink or two, and enjoy the night."

"Thank you, Amina, for that wonderful welcome and everything you do on behalf of the Chicago Bulls," the emcee said.

Nathan's eyes followed her as she walked off the stage. "Damn, Shawn, who was that? She's beautiful!"

"She works with the Bulls on community outreach or something like that. She's here every year. I think she's the one who organizes everything for the gala. She's kind of stuck up. Why? You think you have a shot?"

Nathan smiled. "I don't know if I have a shot, but I would love to at least buy her a drink and see what happens." He had to see for himself if her skin glowed up close.

He scanned the room and found Amina as some guy

came up to her. He had a horrific comb-over and a tan suit two sizes too small. Surely this guy wasn't her date. He grabbed Amina's arm, leaned into her face, and she backed up. He tried to grab her again, but she pulled away; her eyes narrowed at the man who stood in front of her. *If I were this guy, I would run for the hills.* But the creepy guy wouldn't give up. He still tried to force a conversation on her.

Nathan wanted to help her in any way he could. He ordered two glasses of red wine and walked across the room.

WHAT WOULD HAPPEN if she punched this guy in the face? Angela was a few drinks in and flirting her ass off. Amina was on her own. She cocked back her hand as a handsome man approached them.

"There you are. I was looking for you everywhere. You did such an amazing job up there." Nathan smiled.

Amina was stunned but she'd play along to get this creepy guy away from her. "I'm right here." Her voice wasn't her own. She tried to look this handsome stranger in the face but didn't want to stare. He was tall, with fluffy dark hair that connected to his beard. "Thanks for grabbing me a glass of wine."

Nathan leaned down and whispered in Amina's ear, "I saw what was happening, and I planned a rescue mission." He grinned and winked at her.

She felt the scruff of his beard against her skin, and her

body prickled with heat.

Amina grabbed the glass of wine and Nathan's hand. "If you would excuse us," she said to the creepy guy.

They walked away, found a table, and sat down.

"Thank you so much! I was wondering how I could use a karate-kid kick without getting fired or messing up my clothes."

Very tall, with a beard groomed to perfection and demanding to be touched, he had gorgeous blue eyes with flecks of green, framed by long eyelashes. His arms wanted to break free from being confined by his tux jacket. His face had sharp angles and a smile that warmed her heart. She was pretty sure underneath his tux was a—Nope, she couldn't let her brain go that far. Amina had never been to attracted to white men before, but the one who sat in front of her was stunning.

"I cannot thank you enough for coming over."

"I saw the second arm grab and felt like I needed to do something."

"Well, I appreciate the help. I'm Amina Wright." A surge of electricity coursed through her body as he reached out and took her hand. His hand felt strong and gentle at the same time.

"Dr. Nathan Moore."

"Well, Dr. Nathan Moore, I owe you. What are you drinking?"

"I'm fine for now with this glass of wine, but I will take

you up on that offer in a few."

"Is this your first gala? After a while, you start to remember faces, and I don't think I've seen yours before." She would've remembered those eyes.

"Yes. I've been to a few, similar to this, but attending this one here in the museum is a first. My friend, Dr. Shawn Atkins has been coming to this event for the last few years. This year I decided to tag along."

"I know Shawn. He has quite the rep around here."

Nathan shifted in his seat nervously.

"So, what kind of doctor are you?"

"I'm an anesthesiologist at the children's hospital."

"You use that line a lot, huh?" She chuckled. "So, how many other women have you saved tonight?"

"Just you."

Amina adjusted herself in her seat as he grinned at her. It was quiet at their table as they sat and listened to music, took in the room, and avoided direct eye contact with each other.

"So, did you come here alone or with a date?" he finally asked.

Angela danced over to their table before she could respond.

"Mina! I've been looking for you everywhere. You looked so great up there! I want to at least have one drink with you before you leave."

"Sorry, but I was whisked away by my savior here." She pointed to Nathan.

Angela glanced over at him, and a massive grin broke out on her face. Amina introduced her best friend to Nathan, but his eyes never left Amina's gaze.

"So, what's the story? What happened?" Angela continued to smile at them both.

Both Amina and Nathan explained what happened with the guy who didn't know how a lady should be treated.

"I saw that guy on the other side of the band. He seems to be doing that to every woman in the room." Angela leaned her hip against the table. "Glad you were able to be there to help her out."

"It was my pleasure."

Pleasure rolled off his tongue, and Amina tried to stay composed.

"Now we're just sitting here hanging out. I'm waiting for him to tell me what he wants." She knew what she wanted. "I owe him a drink." A waiter strolled by, and she ordered an old-fashioned for him.

"How much longer are you going to stay, Mina?" Angela asked.

"I'm not sure."

"Why do you leave so early?" he asked.

"I enjoy seeing all of the people who contributed and everything, but getting dressed up in the heels just isn't my sort of thing."

"I hear you. I didn't plan on being here that long either, but I'm glad I stayed." Nathan smiled at her. Surely, she was blushing.

"I didn't even realize that people dance at this thing." She laughed. "I thought I got the DJ just for the atmosphere."

"Would you mind dancing with me later?"

"You know, I'm not a big fan of the music playing. I'm sorry."

Angela pulled on Amina's dress. "Nathan, could you excuse Amina and me? I have to go to the ladies' room. Us girls have to stick together."

Once they left out of the ballroom, Angela was filled with questions.

"Okay, Mina, please tell me you are thinking with other parts of your body and not your head."

"Angela!" Amina yelled.

"The thought must've crossed your mind."

"There is no way I'm taking him to my room. I just met him. He is hot, though. And white dudes aren't really my thing." She laughed. "Seriously, though, he's been incredibly kind and nice, but we're just sitting, talking, and enjoying the night, not trying to force anything. We met exactly the way we described it."

Angela interrupted, "Ah, so that means he was watching you. Mina, he looks great, and it seems he likes what he sees in you. Take a chance! Come on!"

"This setting is not the best to try to get to know someone. I'm not even sure if he's dating or what type of person he is."

"Well, he must be pretty decent, to do what he did. If he asks you out, or to see you again, promise me you will say yes. Promise me, Mina." Hope filled her eyes.

"Yes, I promise if he asks but only if he asks. I'm not some desperate woman."

Chapter Three

THE NIGHT TURNED out not to be so bad. Nathan had met a beautiful woman. She bought him a drink, which happened to be his favorite. Now he waited, hoping she'd return, when Shawn finally found him.

"Hey, dude, where you been? I have been looking for you. I met this girl, who's here with her friend. A perfect situation for us both to get lucky if you're interested." Shawn sat down at the table and noticed two wineglasses. He glanced up at Nathan and smiled. "Or did you already find someone else to get lucky with?"

Amina arrived back to the table with Angela, and Nathan was mortified. Shawn was dead if he ruined things for him.

"Who's getting lucky with whom?" Angela asked.

"Hey, ladies, this is my good friend, Dr. Shawn Atkins." Nathan pointed across the table, nervous.

"Hi, Shawn, how are you?" Amina was very curt. "It's good to see you attending another gala. Are you signing up victims—I mean, dates—tonight?"

"It's always a good night," he said.

Amina sat back in her seat across from Nathan and tried to ignore Shawn.

"Nathan, it was nice to meet you. Mina, I will text you later. I'm going to go out there and get my dance on while I can."

Amina hugged her friend and kissed her on the cheek. Shawn left the table, and they were alone.

"I'm sorry for what Shawn said. He can be such an asshole."

"Yeah, that's been my experience. But, it seems like you're not that kind of guy. I mean, not too many assholes are coming up to save women from unsavory guys. They are the unsavory guys."

Nathan smiled.

She had another glass of wine, studying him while she sipped. "I'm sorry that I'm not up for dancing, but feel free to go and dance if you want."

"I'm fine right where I am. What do you like to listen to?"

"Big into indie music," she nervously replied.

Nate nodded. "That's pretty cool." She was so different from any other woman he had ever known. Most women he met were into everything they heard that was popular, but Amina wasn't.

Her director walked over to their table, and their quiet bubble was disrupted.

"Hey, I'll be right back. He needs me to go and take

some pictures. Will you still be here?"

"Right here." It was hard to hide his grin when he looked at her.

Amina walked away to a large group of families who had children who stayed at the children's hospital. He watched her as she shook hands and smiled for pictures.

"Sorry about that," Amina said as she sat back down. "It seems you have a bit of a fan club over there." She motioned her head over to the table filled with beautiful young ladies.

"I had no idea." Nathan was unfazed and uninterested.

"Is that right?"

"Shawn mentioned that he'd seen you here the last few years."

"Yes, this is my baby." Amina motioned her hands around the room. "I work with a team of folks, and we put this on. For the last few years, it's been the event that most people seem to look forward to, and it raises the most money."

"So why do you leave so soon?" He nudged her hands and laughed.

"I don't know. I mean, I do enjoy seeing it all come to-gether. I guess it's that I see a lot of these people enough on a day-to-day basis. Like I said earlier, this whole getting fancy thing; it's just not me. So if I don't have to do it for too long, I won't."

"Well, you look quite beautiful."

"You know I'm exhausted. I think I'm going to head out,

and maybe I can still catch SVP on *Sportscenter* before I turn in."

Nathan was surprised. "Really?"

"Yes. I can't go to sleep at night without watching."

"I don't think I've ever met anyone else who does that." Nathan stroked his beard and grinned while he stared at Amina. He couldn't believe his ears, that someone had an infinity for sports the way he did.

Shawn reappeared at the table. "Wait, you watch *Sportscenter*?"

"Every night and every morning."

"For what?" Shawn asked, stunned.

Nathan stroked his furrowed eyebrow, embarrassed.

"Shawn." Amina smiled at him. "Can you please leave us alone?"

"I'm just making sure my boy here is okay."

"I'm more than okay." Nathan winked.

Shawn put his hands up and walked away.

"What does he think I'm going to do to you?" Amina giggled.

"I haven't been out much lately."

A moment of silence filled their space as they glanced at each other from across the small table. Fingers inched apart, afraid of what to do next.

"So, you're single?" she asked.

"Yep." He exhaled and leaned back, happy she asked. "What hotel are you staying at?"

Amina frowned.

"I'm not asking you to be a weirdo, but just to make sure you get back there safely. Maybe get you an Uber."

"Oh, I'm at the Drake, so not too far, and I should be fine. I can get my own Uber, but thank you."

"Well, can I walk you to the coat check or outside? I'd like to stay with you just in case that tan suit guy comes back."

"Good thinking, Nathan. Yes, that would be fine."

"You can call me Nate, by the way."

"Oh, okay. Good thinking, Nate."

They held hands as they walked out of the main hall. He liked how her hand felt in his; it felt natural. While she got her coat, he ordered an Uber for her. Shawn texted him messages filled with inappropriate nonsense, and Nate knew he saw them when they walked out. She came back to him, and she smiled up at him. He stared back at her and her striking brown skin and gorgeous brown eyes.

"I would like to sit down and talk to you when we're not in such a crowded and busy room. When we're not running away from weird guys and we don't have to shout at each other."

Amina reached her hand out, and Nate gave her his phone. She quickly added her contact info, and he immediately texted her so she would have his number.

"Well, tomorrow I'm busy. I watch college football with my dad most of the day, but Sunday is wide open."

THERE YOU ARE

"Who are you watching?"

"Obviously, the only school that matters, the University of Michigan." She chuckled.

"Wildcat." He laughed with her.

"I'll try not to hold that against you. Is Sunday okay to meet for a late lunch or early dinner?"

"Sure, we can play it by ear." Nate took Amina's hand, and they walked to the exit. When they made it outside, her Uber arrived.

"Thanks so much for everything you did tonight. I hope I didn't ruin your night by leaving early."

"Not at all. I ended up having a perfect time tonight." He smiled.

"Me too." She reached up and kissed the beard that graced his cheek good-night. He closed her car door, and she was gone.

He was about to go back inside and meet Shawn but decided to head home.

When Nate got home, he turned on *Sportscenter*. Had Amina made it back to her hotel? His mind went into a bit of panic—had he put her in a bad situation? What if the creepy guy had followed her to the hotel?

Nate hopped in the shower. Hopefully, it would calm him down and clear his head. He came out, and he grabbed his phone to see if she decided to text him, and he was surprised there was a message.

Are you watching SVP? Are you still at the gala? Sorry if I made you leave earlier than you wanted. Thanks again for everything tonight.

He would owe Shawn big-time. For days he aggravated Nate, and pushed to him to come out for the night. Nate was thrilled that he did.

You are welcome, glad I was able to help. Yes, I made it home. I left right after you left. I am watching SVP right now. So thank you. Any thoughts on what we should do Sunday or where we should go?

I live by a ton of restaurants. What's your favorite kind of food?

Any kind! It doesn't matter, open to anything. Can I come to your place around 5? Just wondering, did you run into the creepy guy?

Ha! Yes! I ended up on an elevator with him! But I got off two floors before my actual stop so he wouldn't know what level I was on. Five sounds perfect. I'm exhausted, so I will see you Sunday. Thanks again for everything, Nate. Have a good night.

You too, Amina. Good night.

Chapter Four

THE BRIGHT SUN and blaring city sounds woke Amina in her hotel room. She was a little hungover and drained. Was Nathan a figment of her imagination? Was he too good to be true? A knock at the door shook the vision of Nate from her mind. Angela sauntered in with a much-needed coffee in her hand. Nothing was packed in Amina's room, and they had to make the check-out time.

"So, what happened with you and the hot superhero doctor?" Angela asked while they threw clothing into a suitcase.

Amina laughed; he was real. "Well, he didn't come back to my room if that's what you want to know. But I do have a date with him tomorrow evening."

"Okay, Mina, okay, I see you." Angela high-fived her. "Dating is much different now than it was years ago. You need to loosen up."

"Angie, I will not be giving him any on the first date, like that's not happening. I can't go out like that. Nope, not doing it." She shook her head and laughed.

"You're saying that now." Angela put her arm across

Amina's shoulders. "But it's going to come down to the end of the night. He's going to be looking at you with those eyes. I'm just saying I won't be mad at you if you did. Are you ready for something like this? I mean, you have never gone out with someone who looks like Nathan."

"You mean as hot as him." Amina laughed, but she knew what Angela was getting at. "I haven't really thought about it. Well, maybe a little bit. It's definitely outside of my comfort zone for sure. But he was so kind." Amina didn't want to miss out on something special just because of his race. She just wasn't sure if she was up for this kind of challenge.

"Are you still going over to your dad's?"

"Heading there now. Kickoff is at noon."

"All right, well, give him my love, please."

"Will do." They went down to the lobby, checked out, and hugged each other goodbye.

"Mina, you better text me and let me know how your date goes," Angela shouted as she walked away.

When Amina arrived at Dad's flat, he was on the couch, waiting for her. His apartment was filled with pictures of her, her brother, Amir, and photos from the years Dad had performed with his jazz band. Their mother left them when Amir was five, and she was three. No reason, no explanation; she just left. Dad couldn't be out there on the road with two small kids, so he had to stop doing what he loved and raise them. He worked odd jobs to get by, but he got back in school. Became a manager of a manufacturing company, but he never stopped playing. Music was his first love. As soon as they were able to manage themselves on their own, he was able to perform again, and it was like he had never stopped.

In the last six years, her dad battled various forms of cancers. He had reached the point where treatment was not an option. It was only a matter of time. Amina had come to his apartment and watched Michigan football games with him every single Saturday during the season for the last six years. She'd attended the Michigan football games with her father as a little girl, and she fell in love with the school. When it was time for her to go to college, there was only one choice.

He patted the spot next to him on the couch.

"Hey, Daddy." He was a bit thinner than he was last week.

"Hey, baby girl, how are you?"

"I'm good, a little tired."

"Oh yeah, your big party was last night. How did everything go?" His voice was a little weak too.

"It went well. I ended up having a great time."

"Well, tell me all about it."

Tina, his caregiver, stuck her head in from the kitchen. "Mina, I'm going to run some errands. I should be back in a couple of hours." Tina had been a lifesaver, making sure everything was taken care of for him.

"Okay, Tina, thanks so much."

He still ate and drank on his own, which Amina was

happy to see. Her phone vibrated in her lap.

A pretty boring game so far, huh?

Her heart fluttered in her chest while she read the message from Nate.

My dad was just complaining about that; he'll probably be asleep soon if things don't pick up. How are you?
Pretty good, little hungover, but good. You?
Same.

She grinned from ear to ear as they texted back and forth. Her body tingled all over as she thought about his handsome face and that grin of his.

Her dad looked at her, annoyed. "Did you come over here to watch the game with me or to sit and type on that thing? And what's the story? Who's making you smile like that?"

Caught, gotta go.
See you tomorrow.

"Well, Daddy, if you must know, I was texting with a nice man I met at the fancy party last night."

He perked up, and Amina appreciated she was able to talk to him about anything. She told her dad what happened with the man in the tan suit, and how Nate came to her rescue.

"That's pretty stand-up of Nate, and smart. I know you

were ready to hit Mr. Pushy."

"You know I was, Daddy." She giggled.

"What does he do?"

"He's an anesthesiologist at the Robert Lurie Children's Hospital."

Her dad nodded, impressed. "White guy?"

Amina wasn't sure how he figured that out. "Yeah." She looked at the ground, afraid to meet her father's eyes.

Amina was always so proud of who she was, and her father made sure of that. She wasn't sure how he would receive the idea of her considering going out with someone who was white. He had such little time left, and the last thing she wanted was to be a disappointment.

His brow furrowed. What was he thinking?

He nodded. "Well, are you going to see him again?"

"Tomorrow evening." Thank God he wasn't angry.

"Well, I'm not going to tell you who you can and cannot date. You are a grown and smart woman. What I will tell you is, of course, that's not my wish for you. When I imagine who you are going to grow old with, I picture someone with a bit more melanin in their skin. I mean, is that something you think you're ready for? Stares and whispers and who knows what else? Just make sure you fully understand what the weight of that means, and the fallout that could come from it all."

"I will think about all of that. It's just he was so kind. But, honestly, Dad, I didn't think too much about it." The warmth Amina felt disappeared with his words, but she appreciated his frankness; it provided her with some perspective that maybe she didn't see.

"Where did he go to school?" Dad asked.

"He's a Wildcat."

"Okay, well, as long as he ain't no Buckeye, he's fine. So he has that going for him." He laughed.

Her father fell asleep midway through the fourth quarter.

ANGELA CALLED HER when she got in her car. "Are you still out?"

"Yeah, just leaving my dad's. What's up?"

"Me and Lisa are about to meet up at the Milk Room for drinks."

"There's no weird dress code or anything, is there?" She was dressed in a T-shirt, track jacket, jeans, Jordans, and her locs flowed free.

"Nope, no dress code."

"Okay, I'll meet you guys there."

Amina walked into the bar, spotted them at a table, and hugged them both. "I was just catching Lisa up on last night," Angela said.

"Yes, Mina, it sounds like you hit the jackpot."

"Well, we'll see. I'm meeting him tomorrow. So we'll see how things go."

"Girl, he is fine as hell!" Angela pulled out her phone and

showed Lisa a picture of Nate and Amina.

"Damn, Mina. He is hot. Stop trying to downplay it." Lisa laughed.

Amina grabbed a seat. Hopefully, the night wasn't going to be filled with them picking on her. She wasn't in the mood for their shit. She was already second-guessing every moment of seeing Nate again. Her father's words had struck a nerve.

"Anyway, Lisa, what's going on? I thought you were coming last night. What happened?"

"Girl, Zion got sick, so I had to stay and take care of him. Sorry I couldn't make it. It sounds like I missed a good time."

"You have got to be kidding me." Angela looked at the bar.

"What, what's wrong, Angie?"

"Lisa, does that guy at the bar look like the guy I just showed you on my phone? Don't look now. Okay, look."

Lisa looked over. "Yeah, that's your guy, Mina." Lisa grinned.

"Okay, first of all, that's not my guy. Second of all, this is weird as hell." Amina couldn't wrap her brain around it all before she realized Angela was gone.

She pointed Nate and whoever his friend was over to their table. He looked terrific in his bomber jacket, V-neck shirt, jeans, and sneakers. He smiled and waved at her.

Nate and his friend strolled over to their table. "Hey,

ladies, how are you?" He disarmed them all with his charm. "This is my good friend, Chris."

"Nice to meet everyone." Chris waved.

"Chris, you know, I heard there's an enclosed rooftop bar upstairs," Angela said. "It's supposed to be nice. We should go check it out." And with that, her friends left the table in the most ungraceful way possible.

"She was a tad bit obvious." Nate smiled and sat down across from her.

"Just a bit." Amina peered over at him and the V-neck opening of his shirt. A bit of his muscle peeked out.

"You look great."

"Thanks." Amina ignored the heat that rose beneath her skin. "So, are you spying on me or what?"

He laughed. "No! Absolutely not! I was at home with Chris, and we were watching games. I don't live too far away, and we wanted to go out for a drink to catch up a bit. That's all. I saw you when we walked in, and I purposely did not come over here. Because it would've seemed weird, right?"

She nodded.

"Exactly, so we just went to the bar, then Angela came over. So please, relax. I'm not spying on you or anything like that. But, it is nice to see you."

Her body clenched with desire. All her little nagging doubts she had about him were drifting further away.

"Should we go upstairs and join them?" She needed some

fresh air.

He gently took her hand. "Hang on a sec. How was your day with your dad?"

"It was good. He thinks you're nice, by the way, but that you might not want to try that move on too many more women, though."

He laughed.

"I left before the game was over, though."

"Do you want to know it ended?"

"I caught it on the radio. I know Michigan won. How'd your Wildcats do?" She smirked.

"Okay, now we can go and join them." Nate laughed.

"ALL RIGHT, YOU guys, I'm done. I'm going home." Amina hadn't laughed like that in a long time.

"Oh, come on, Mina. Please stay longer," Lisa said.

"It's already late, and I'm exhausted. No, I'm gone." Amina hugged her friends, and suddenly Nate was at her side.

"Nate, I can walk to my car. I'm fine."

"I know. I just wanted to make sure you get there with no problem. Is that okay?"

"Yeah, that's fine." She'd expected at least another day before she was alone with him. Amina felt the sweat on her palms.

The crisp fall air greeted them when they stepped outside

of the bar. Her voice was filled with nerves. "I parked a few blocks away, so we don't have to walk too far. Tomorrow, it'll be nice to talk to you without an audience."

He chuckled. "Yes. Looking forward to that."

They arrived at her car, and he moved close. He placed his hand against her waist. Amina imagined his firm, soft hands on other parts of her body as he whispered, "It was great running into you tonight."

"You know, once I knew you weren't some weirdo, it was nice seeing you too."

He moved closer, and she felt his breath against her skin.

"So, I'll see you tomorrow at five."

"At five. I'll text you tomorrow to get your address." He grinned and opened her door.

"Good night, Nate."

AMINA CLEANED HER house like a crazy woman. She didn't want Nate to think she lived like some kind of a slob. After the way he'd put his hand on her waist and that smile…her stomach churned with anticipation. She couldn't believe that he had this type of effect on her.

She went to her closet next. What the hell was she going to wear? She had to call Angela for some sage advice.

"Hey, he's coming at five to pick me up for dinner. I'm freaking out!" Amina pulled her legs to her chest as she sat on her bed.

"Okay, good! Wear cute underwear."

"Angela!" she yelled into the phone. "I just needed some reassurance. That's all. You know I haven't been out on a date in a while, and it seems like tonight could be a good one. I don't want to ruin it." She leaned her head back against her pillow.

"At the bar last night, you could've been wearing a paper bag and he would've gladly sat and enjoyed being with you in that paper bag. He wants to spend time with you. Otherwise, none of what happened Friday night or last night would have happened. So, just put on what makes you feel the most like you. Do your hair and makeup, and have a good time."

Amina relaxed. "Thanks, Ang. I will text you and let you know how the night goes."

"Or text me tomorrow and let me know how the night went." Angela cackled.

"Love you, Angie, and kiss David for me. Tell him we're still on for our date night in a couple of weeks."

Amina lit candles and got ready. She followed her best friend's advice—*dress like yourself.* She put on her favorite jeans, a cute, fitted sweater perfect for the fall weather, and a pair of sneakers. She checked her hair, made sure her makeup was flawless but as natural as possible.

Her phone disrupted her chill mood. "Hello."

"Hey, Amina, it's Nate. I should be there in about fifteen minutes."

She hadn't realized how deep his voice was. It must've been the loudness from the bar or the crowd at the gala, but she heard it now.

"Okay, I have a driveway, so don't worry about looking for a place to park."

"Great. I look forward to seeing you soon."

How had she missed the sexiness in his voice and the calmness? *Focus, Amina, focus. No matter what, not on the first night.*

Chapter Five

WHY HADN'T HE kissed her good-night at her car? She stood in front on him with a smile as bright as the sunshine. Feeling her full lips against his, to feel her body pressed against his was all he wanted. It would've been amazing. If he got the opportunity, he wouldn't let that slip away again.

He rang her doorbell.

She came to the door, and her skin looked like it was kissed by the sun.

"Hey, did you find the house okay? It can be a little confusing."

"Yeah, I found it with no problems. Glad you have a driveway because parking would've been tough." He walked past her into her foyer and studied the painting that hung on the wall. He pulled off his jacket and placed it across his arm.

Amina's eyes followed every move he made.

"It's nice to see you again," he said.

"You too."

They hugged and stood in silence.

She shrugged and blew air out of her cheeks. "Well, let me show you around the house."

It was a decent-sized three-bedroom home. There was a staircase that greeted him when he walked in, with the living room on one side and the dining room on the other. Her house was decorated with lots of neutral tones, with artwork and pictures lining the walls. Soft music played in every room, and it smelled like amber. But she kept him on the first floor.

"The zoo's not too far from you." His voice boomed through her kitchen.

"Not too far at all. When David comes over in the summer, we walk over."

"And who's David?"

"Oh, that's Angela's son. That's my little buddy." She sat down at her dining room table and offered him a seat.

"So, what type of restaurants are around here?"

"Are we going to drive?"

"It's a pretty nice night to walk if we're not going too far."

"There's this charming Italian restaurant a few blocks from here, great food, quiet, good wine. Angela and I found it a little after I moved into the neighborhood. It is sort of just sitting there, unnoticed."

"Sounds perfect."

"Let me just grab a few things, and we can go."

The restaurant was tiny and quaint with candle centerpieces at each table. They grabbed a table and ordered a bottle of wine.

Nate squirmed in his seat and kept pulling at the cuffs of his shirt. The waiter placed a plate of warm, fresh bread on the table. Nate reached for his knife, and it tumbled to the floor, making every eye in the restaurant turn to them.

"Are you okay?" Amina asked. "You seem like something is wrong."

He sighed. "Can I be honest?"

"Please."

"I'm just nervous. Being in the presence of a beautiful woman has that kind of effect on me."

Amina laughed. "I was so nervous about tonight. It feels so much like a high school first date. We have to get it together here." She smiled.

He took a deep breath. Amina was stunning, even more beautiful than the night they met. It was hard not to imagine being alone with her in this restaurant and placing her on one of these tables and kissing her everywhere he could.

Be cool.

"When was the last time you were out on a date like this?" he asked.

"Don't laugh, okay. It's been about two years."

"You're lying." He couldn't understand why men wouldn't be lined up to take her out.

"I'm dead serious. Two years. Your turn."

He glanced down and whispered, "Two years."

"We are such a mess." She smirked.

They ordered their food and she stared across the table. "Why has it been so long?"

"Well, I had a bad breakup. Not sure I want to get into all of that right at this moment if that's okay?"

She nodded.

"Then I got very busy with work. I know that sounds like such a cliché thing to say, but I did. I became the lead anesthesiologist and started mentoring younger doctors like Shawn, and that's been cool. You look up and two years have passed. You meet this beautiful woman, you ask her out, and she says yes. You kind of forget how to act."

He smiled at her when she laughed.

"So, how did you know you wanted to be a doctor?"

"Well, I knew when I was like twelve or thirteen. I was a bit of a nerdy kid." He grinned. "I always loved science and wanted to help kids. One day, I was playing basketball in the neighborhood when my best friend at the time landed really awkwardly, and he ended up breaking his ankle. We had to carry him back home, and he was crying in pain and so scared. I remember seeing how he was treated at the hospital. How calm and cool the doctors were to him. How they took care of him. I wanted to do that. I wanted kids to look up to me, and to take excellent care of them. Plus, you know, I'm a bit of a big kid anyway, so being at the children's hospital is perfect."

Nathan leaned across the table to be as close as he could

to Amina. He was so at ease talking to her, and she looked striking as she sat across from him next to the candlelight.

"I started in ortho, and I didn't really like that, and then I moved to vascular surgery. I didn't like that either. I felt like I needed to take a break to figure out what I truly wanted to do with medicine. To find out if this was something I still really wanted to pursue, you know? You have a dream for so long, by the time you're in it, it might not feel the same."

"That makes sense."

"So, I traveled for a year with my dad. I came back and decided I could be in every surgery as an anesthesiologist. Sometimes with an operation, your doctor can be in such a rush to get you in and get you out. I could be the last person families and kids talked to before they went into surgery. I liked that better. These kids and families are so scared, you know?"

"You do have this calming way about you."

"Thanks." He smiled sheepishly.

Nate wasn't ready for the night to end. He was having such a good time being with her. He had to figure out how to extend their time together.

"Amina, after dinner, do you think we could get some dessert?"

Nate sat and waited for her response, and she said nothing.

"Amina, did you hear what I said?"

"I'm sorry, Nate. What were you saying?"

"I was asking if, after dinner, you wanted to grab dessert. If that's okay?"

She grabbed his hands and gazed in his eyes. "I'm sorry. I was just daydreaming about something. What you're doing as a doctor sounds very noble, and you should be very proud of yourself. Yes, I would love dessert after dinner."

"Any ideas?" Nate helped with her jacket.

"There's a bakery just down the way. They're open until midnight. Now that weed is legal, these smart college kids got together and opened up this bakery. The donuts there are amazing. Seriously amazing. I'm not sure they don't have weed in them, with how much you keep wanting to go back and get more."

He laughed at how animated she was talking about these donuts. "All right, we'll go to the bakery. Sounds good."

Amina held his hand as they walked down the street.

They debated Lebron's many moves, Steph's lack of final MVPs, and KD's legacy. He fed off her spirit and her energy, and he wanted more and more of it.

"Where did this love for ball come from?" he asked.

"My dad. I grew up in a house with all men, and he had to find ways to keep me entertained. Basketball and Michigan football was how we bonded and how we've remained so close. Working for the Bulls is a dream job."

"He must be proud."

"He tells me he is all the time." She smiled. "Nate, why

has no one snatched you up yet? Like you're this sweet, handsome guy who wants to be the calming voice kids hear before scary operations. Women must be throwing themselves at you all day. How are you not married?"

He loosened his hand around hers and then it tightened again. How could he explain that he wasn't interested in being hurt again? He didn't want her to think he was weak. Explaining that to her was a tough thing to do. He didn't know what she was looking for. Was spilling his guts even worth it?

She tugged on his jacket and peeked up at him.

He rubbed his thumb over her hand. "You know that's a good question, a fair question. I'll answer it, but can we get our donuts first? Can we take them back to your place, and I'll answer all of these questions there?"

"Sure, that's fair."

Nate nodded. What, exactly, was he going to tell her?

Chapter Six

"You promise you're not about to tell me you keep your ex-girlfriend's nail clippings or something?"

"Just the hair clippings," he joked. "No, it's not that bad, but the story is sort of long, too long to stay at a bakery to tell," he said.

"Sure, anything to get back to my house. I see how it is." Amina chuckled.

She took his jacket as they walked inside, and he was surprised she hung it up for him. He took the donuts and the coffees into the living room and waited for her.

"Hey, sorry about that. Angela and I have this thing when we go out on a date we have a list of random words we text to each other to let the other person know we're okay. We have to leave the room to do it, just in case the guy is looking over our shoulder or something strange is going on, you know?"

"That's a cool and smart idea. I wasn't sure, shoes on or off?"

"I don't care, whatever."

He walked to her foyer and placed his shoes next to hers. The sounds of a guitar strumming and a piano filled her home. It was music he never heard before, calm, unique, just like her.

Amina took a seat on the couch and sat with one foot underneath her. She had a donut in her hand, and she patted the space next to her on the couch.

"Okay, what's the tea? Why are you single?"

He laughed. "The tea, huh?"

"Yes, tea." She grinned.

"All right, so in high school, I dated this girl, Stacy, my senior year. Of course, we felt like we were madly in love. Went to prom together, were each other's first, all of that. When it came time to apply to colleges, we ended up applying to the same schools. We got into all of them, but we decided on Northwestern."

She booed and gave him a thumbs-down, and he laughed.

"I applied to med school at Northwestern to make sure that we could stay together. I could've gone somewhere else, but she was important to me, and it seemed like the right thing to do, you know? Things were going well. We found a place together, got a dog, all of that, she graduated, started an internship. Life was good."

"Both of you still madly in love and faithful?" she asked.

"Yes, of course. I'm not the cheating kind of guy. It's something I've never fully understood. The idea of someone cheating. If things are that bad or you're bored, just say something. Anyway." Nate shook his head and exhaled after taking a deep breath.

"I started my residency, working a lot of hours. She started to feel a bit neglected. So I felt like I needed to do something drastic to make her feel special." He glanced at her; he inhaled the scent of her skin and realized how close she was to him.

"What did you do?" she asked.

"Well, I asked her to marry me."

"Wow!" She laughed.

"I know, I know. It was kinda stupid, considering we never discussed it. All that time together, and we just never really talked about any of that stuff. Anyway, there's more to the story."

"Okay." She folded her other leg underneath her on the couch.

"So, I asked her to marry me. Mind you; I had no ring. So the next day, we went and picked it out. I picked out something much smaller than what she wanted, which made her very unhappy. But she was still super excited about getting married. We told our parents, and we had an engagement party and everything. The plan was I would finish my residency before the wedding."

Amina nodded.

"So, one day, I came home from a rotation, was up all night and needed to shower—you know, change clothes get back to the hospital. What do I find?"

"No way!" she shouted.

"Yes! Stacy was getting it on, in our bed with a guy from pickup basketball. I didn't even know they knew each other."

"That's quite the story, Nate."

He exhaled and leaned his head back. "The thing is, I felt so relieved."

"You both knew it was a bad idea. What happened after you caught them?"

"Well, she moved out. At first, I was really lonely. Coming home and no one was there—it was strange. After a while, I adjusted, and threw myself into work. I finished my residency. Then all the stuff I told you about me taking some time off. This sort of played a role in it. My head was screwed up a little bit."

"I bet. I mean, that's a lot of time you invested in someone, and then for them to just throw that away, and not talk to you. But you didn't talk to her either, so." She shrugged.

"She ended up marrying the guy from pickup basketball."

"Are you serious?"

"So crazy. It happened quickly too." He hesitated.

"There's more. Spill."

He smiled. "I went through a phase after I caught them. I tried to be this like player guy."

Amina snickered. "That doesn't even seem like you at all."

"It's not. I'm much more of a relationship guy. I would go out with women, and after a few dates, I wanted something more serious. I think I was moving too fast, and that scared them away."

"Yeah, I could see that. So, is this when you started trying to figure out your next move?" she asked.

"Yeah. I decided not to date and focus on medicine. I was getting used to being alone. I was not in the best headspace, you know? Going to the gala was a big deal for me. It was the first time I had been out in a while. That's why Shawn was acting the way he was. It all worked out, and I'm pleased I went." He paused and stared at her.

"Do you still talk to Stacy?"

"Not really. Things ended pretty badly. I see Corey every now and again, when we play ball, but aside from that, she and I don't speak." Nate glanced at the clock on the wall. "Oh damn, Amina, I didn't realize how late it was. I have to be at the hospital in a few hours."

"I'm so sorry. I didn't mean to keep you out so late."

"No need to apologize. I had such a good time tonight."

"Me too."

"Those donuts were amazing, by the way."

"Right? It's becoming my favorite thing to eat after dinner. I seriously need to come up with some type of diet plan quickly if I'm going to keep eating there."

"You look fine to me," he said, and Amina blushed.

She stood next to him in the foyer while he put on his

sneakers and then helped him with his coat.

"Can you text me when you get home so that I know you made it safely?" she asked.

"Sure." He wrapped his arms around her, and her body pressed against his.

He'd wanted to do this from the moment he saw her in that black dress. He slid his hands from her waist and gazed into her eyes. Amina rested her fingertips against his chest and he tried to remained composed. He leaned in and kissed her full, soft lips. It was slow and sweet. He pulled her body close to his, and she put her hands in his hair.

She grinned as she drew away from him. "Nate, it's getting later. You have to go if you want to save lives in a few hours."

He smiled and whispered against her neck, "You're right. Good night, Amina." He kissed her on the cheek and walked out the door.

AMINA STOOD AT her window and watched him as he drove away. She went upstairs and took the coldest of cold showers. She climbed into bed and pulled her knees to her chest. Her body screamed for him. She rubbed her thumb against her lips and thought about how he kissed her. All day, her mind had been filled with her father's words. Wondering if she was ready to be involved with someone like Nate. Luckily, after listening to him be so open about his past, she knew that he wasn't ready for anything serious. The type of pain and disappointment he went through just didn't magically disappear.

Still, Amina enjoyed the way he held her body against his and how strong his chest felt beneath her fingertips. She knew precisely what she wanted from him, and hoped things would be heading in that direction. Amina sighed, and she laid her head against the pillow, relieved. This would be nothing more than the fun good time she needed.

AMINA TRIED TO sleep in, but the world wouldn't let her. She still had quite a few loose ends she needed to wrap up from the gala—namely, making sure money was placed where it needed to be, and wondering if it was all to the satisfaction of the Bulls. Yet her mind drifted to Nate and wondering about what was underneath his clothes. She still wasn't sure what he wanted, if this was all just fun. Even though Amina was more than willing to be with him physically, she was sure she wasn't ready for anything more. Was good sex worth all of this?

Her phone rang and startled her. It was her brother, Amir.

"Mir, what's up?"

"Hey, Mina, saw Dad yesterday. He said you were over on Saturday. Glad you made it out."

"I did. I thought you were going to join us."

"I planned on being there, but I had some stuff to do with Cheryl and the kids. He mentioned something about you seeing a white doctor? Is that what we're doing now, sis?" He sounded disappointed.

All the warm sensations Amina felt from thinking of Nate vanished. "Mir, I hope you know I will date or be with who I want. I don't need your approval." She'd have to be ready for this type of judgment.

Her father had already told her he wasn't thrilled. Now Amir. Who knew what everyone else was going to think? Being with Nate could lead people to think she was turning her back on her community, as silly as it sounded. It made her sick that anyone would think that of her, but knowing her dad and brother did was like ice in her veins.

"I know that. I'm just saying."

"What is it that you're saying?" Amina flopped down her couch, annoyed.

"All right." He laughed. "How was the gala? A few of my friends went there. They said it was lit. I know you were pretty worried about it the last time we had dinner with Dad."

"It all turned out really well. Everyone looked like they had a good time. I have a meeting to see how the budget is looking and projections and all of that. Trying not to think about it all."

"Well, I didn't mean to bother you. Just wanted to check in. Do you plan on seeing the doctor again?" he asked.

"Maybe."

"Just be careful, okay, sis?"

"Anything else, sir?"

Her brother laughed. "Just a heads-up. I got a tip. Your ex is lurking around."

Her body went cold. "Thanks, Mir. I will make sure to be safe. I gotta talk to you later."

"Peace."

She hung up and threw her phone across the couch. Her hands shook at the memories of Omar yelling at her. His glare that cut right through her being. She needed to brace herself. Amina rolled over on the sofa. She pulled a blanket over her head while the phone danced underneath her body. She peeked at it. Amina had so much she needed to get done, she wasn't sure she was up for any more judgments so early in the morning.

Good morning! Are you enjoying the day?

Just seeing Nate's name sent her body and her mind in different directions. *Hey, you! How many fears have you calmed today?*

Just a few, still early. Wednesday, are you free? I'd like to cook dinner for you.

Amina wasn't sure what she should do. She did enjoy her time with him, but she still was unclear of what he wanted. Plus, after speaking with Amir, she wasn't sure about adding another layer of stress to her life.

> *Can I get back to you? I'm still wrapping up some things from the gala, not sure how the rest of my day will look.*
>
> *Sure, just let me know.*
>
> *Will do. Thanks, have a great day.*
>
> *You too.*

Amina sat on her couch, clueless. Was she overthinking all of this? Why couldn't she say yes and be with him? Just let go and enjoy what she knew would be a good night. She pulled the blanket over her head and, this time, she envisioned what was underneath Nate's clothes.

Chapter Seven

WEDNESDAY ARRIVED, AND all Amina wanted was to see Nate again. She dreamt of his strong arms lifting her up and gently laying her on his bed, his lips all over her body. She wanted to feel it all. She really didn't care what his plans were. All she wanted was him, every single inch of him.

Good morning. Does my invitation still stand?

Yes, still stands. Is 5 okay?

5 would be perfect.

Great! I'll send you my address and see you then.

Amina's body could not calm down. Visions of his muscles and his lips would not escape her mind. It was hard, but Amina had to refocus on her day. It was filled with calls back to make sure the necessary accounts were funded. She received a call from her boss.

"Hey, Amina, I just wanted to let you know that we were under our goal."

"Yeah, I'm going through some of the final numbers now. And it's not looking good." Her voice was stressed, and she was already tired.

"So, here's what we're going to do. When I come into the office, we're going to refocus our efforts on having small scale events throughout the year. We need to come up with a game plan to figure out how to do that. How to be more visible. Maybe that will work out better for us next year when the gala rolls around."

"That sounds good, Sam. I'll finish up these calls and start fleshing out some ideas on some of our options."

"Great, see you tomorrow."

Amina hung up from her boss and threw herself into her work. She thought of a series of ideas to pitch to him and the president of the Bulls the next day when she returned into the office. All the while fielding texts from Amir to update her on her father's appointments. She finished up her work as Angela strolled through the front door.

"Hey, girl, what's going on?"

"Nothing much, just finishing up work for the day. Then I have to start figuring out what I'm going to wear over to Nate's tonight."

"Keep it casual whatever you do. I would even do a T-shirt and some jeans, with a cute scarf or something."

"Thanks, Angie. He's been pretty open, like shockingly so. When we went out, I asked him about why he was still single. And, he was very open about it all. It was refreshing. He's funny and kind. We had a good time at dinner. And, girl, his voice, it is unnerving how sexy and deep it is! I have

IESHIA WIEDLIN

to keep it together while he's talking. I kind of lose focus sometimes, and I think he notices. It's embarrassing." She laughed.

"Have you told him about Omar yet? And everything that went on with him?" Angela asked.

Amina shivered and sighed. "I'm not sure I'm ready to have that conversation, or if I need to. I don't think this is going to be a very serious thing. So why ruin it?"

"Well, it's probably best to be just as open with him as he's with you. How are you feeling with the race difference? I know you were worried about that." Amina walked with Angela to her kitchen bar and poured a glass of wine.

"Honestly, I had such a good time with him the other night, I didn't think about it. I mean, it's always in the back of my mind, this is all so new to me. It doesn't seem like he's bothered or worried about anything." She sighed.

She wasn't going to let her dad's and brother's words ruin her night. She was taking a chance and just wanted to focus on that.

"I didn't tell you he kissed me—well, we kissed. Right over there." She grinned as she pointed to the foyer.

"Yeah, no, you didn't mention that." Angela punched her in the arm.

"It took all I had to make sure he went home. I couldn't go out like that on the first date. But, girl, it was amazing. His body has got to be sick because his chest felt like I was touching a damn wall."

52

"Tonight is the second date, so…" Angela shrugged.

"Well, the good thing is all the pressure is off. All the awkwardness of the first date is gone, so that makes things a little easier. I mean, I'm nervous, but not as much. I feel like we know each other a bit better now. If it went there, I would be down."

"Pack a bag, Mina." Angela laughed. "And, make sure you text me, to let me know you're good, and just enjoy yourself, Mina, you deserve it. You deserve to be happy. Don't be afraid to just be in the moment."

"Okay. Love you, give David my hugs and kisses."

"Love you too. Mina's gonna get nasty," Angela sang.

"Shut up. Bye. Get out!" She laughed and pushed her friend out the door.

Amina put on a cute, nerdy T-shirt, scarf, jeans, Jordan 1s, and a lovely coat. She packed a bag with a change of clothes and toothbrush, just in case.

Nate lived on the ninth floor of a pretty chic warehouse building off of Lake Shore Drive. Amina drummed her fingers along her steering wheel and rolled her window down, hoping the breeze would cool her overheated body off.

She pulled into the garage and parked in the visitor section. His eyes washed over her as she approached him, waiting by the elevators with his hands in the pockets of his jeans. His fluffy hair was perfect. Not a strand was out of place, and his beard was freshly trimmed.

Holy shit, he looked good.

"Hey, you." She waved as he grinned.

"Hey." He hugged, kissed her on the cheek.

She felt his breath, and as his beard grazed against her skin, her body ignited. "I'm very interested to see how a doctor lives."

"I'm sure I live just like everybody else. I mean, with the addition of a few cool things here and there." He winked.

His loft was huge. The layout was of exposed brick and beams with floor-to-ceiling windows. The living room had a massive couch that sat in front of a fireplace with a television above it. A balcony overlooked the dining room and living room. With a dream kitchen as a centerpiece of the room, it was gorgeous. The color scheme was a soft orange and neutral tones.

A winding staircase led to his bedroom.

He smiled as he watched her walk around, checking things out.

"I would offer you a drink, but I can't have anything just in case I have to go in to the hospital."

"Oh, that's right. You're on call." She felt deflated. She hoped he didn't realize. "What smells so good?"

"I made you my most favorite thing, and I hope it becomes your favorite thing." He stood behind the island in his kitchen, excited.

"Oh yeah, what's that?"

"Chicken parmigiana. I made it from my mom's recipe.

It's probably the only thing I trust myself to make for someone else."

The dining room table was set, salad, warm bread, main course, everything looked so great.

"No music playing?" she asked.

"I wasn't sure what you wanted to listen to."

"Surprise me."

He grabbed his phone, and a sultry singer's voice filled the room.

"Nicely done." Amina grinned at him.

She was so ready for wherever the night was headed.

"Nate, the food is so good. And you're right. This might be my new favorite thing."

He smiled at her, pleased with himself.

"I hope you're not bothered by the question I'm about to ask, but it's something I need to know," she said after she sipped her water and dug her fork back into her plate.

"Shoot."

"Have you ever dated a Black woman before?" Amina's palms began to sweat.

The last thing she wanted was to be someone's experiment. Amina needed to know if he would know how to navigate this new reality.

Nate put his fork down and smirked at her. "I was wondering when this was gonna come up. Yes, I have, for a little bit after Stacy. This isn't new for me. Is this new for you? Going out with someone white?"

Amina nodded. She was incredibly attracted to him, but she had to admit, to herself at least, she was scared.

"To say I'm blind to it would be foolish. I know the looks and stares. I get it. I could also get the fear around it, too, but I hope that it's something you can deal with."

Amina was quiet and unsure of what to say next. Hopefully, she hadn't ruined the night. He walked over, took her hands, stood her up, and they danced. She put her hands on his chest. The muscles begged to be touched. He leaned in close and placed his hand on her face. He stroked her cheek with his thumb. Her body was screaming for him, and she didn't give a damn about the color of his skin.

"Dammit." He sighed as his phone rang. He kissed her and answered the phone. "Dr. Moore."

Amina chuckled as he walked away. She had never seen him in doctor mode, and it was sexy as hell. She grabbed the plates, cleared the table.

"Are you sure?" he said. "Well, I'm free to come in if I'm needed. Oh, okay, how's she doing? That's good, that's good. Dr. Heller came in? Yeah, I see. Sure, that's fine. Well, I'm here. Sounds good. I'll probably come in earlier tomorrow to check over everything then."

She tried to follow the conversation and load the dishwasher at the same time, but she gave up.

Nate finally hung up. "Good news, another doctor took over services for the night. They took me off the on-call list, so I'm free for the night."

"That's great." Her body was still overheated from being in his arms.

She wanted more of him.

He took a bottle of wine from the chiller. "Did you want a glass?"

"Yes, please."

"I almost forgot. I have a surprise for dessert." Nate pulled out a bag of donuts from her bakery, with bacon-covered donuts inside.

"This is incredible, thanks." She kissed his cheek.

They walked over to his couch and sat down.

"Is everything okay?" she asked.

"Yeah, I was just added to a surgery team for a girl named Ryan. The doctor who took over for the night just filled me in on everything. Gave me an idea of what to expect tomorrow. How was your day?" He put his arm around her against the couch, and Amina happily set her head against it.

"It was good. Just planning what the next move will be. The projections for the gala fell short, so we have to figure out some smaller things. Maybe more small camps with the players, meet and greets. Have to figure out the next best move for the team and all the community services the team will be doing with some of the schools." She looked over to him, and took in the mole on his neck, and the plumpness of his lips.

His body felt so warm sitting next to hers, and she felt

the flex of his biceps behind her. Amina set her wineglass down on the coffee table. She leaned over and kissed him, her fingers stroking his beard while her lips moved against his.

He pulled her onto his lap with his hands at her waist. "I wanted to do this the moment you walked out of your car," he whispered when he broke away for a moment.

"Me too." Amina grinned at him.

They kissed again, and Nate moved to her neck, and she raked her fingers through his hair. He lifted her from his lap, held her hand, and led her up the stairs to his bedroom. It was huge. Amina bit her lip in anticipation when she saw the dark-colored covers on his bed; she couldn't wait to be wrapped up in the sheets with him.

She felt his breath on the back of her neck, and she turned around. Nate placed his hand on her face and kissed her again. He took off Amina's shirt and smiled like he'd unwrapped the gift he wanted the most for Christmas.

"You seem to like what you see," Amina said to him as she laughed.

"I do." He nodded as he grinned. "I really do."

She took off his black Henley, and damn, he was everything she imagined and dreamed. His skin was flawless, and his chest was perfect. She placed her hands on it and kissed him. She stood and traced her fingers across his body. Down and across his abs, and she smiled as he responded to her touch. How many hours did he spend working out to look this way? Honestly, she didn't care, but she was grateful he did.

She moved her fingers across the top of his jeans and grinned with anticipation.

Nate lifted her and placed her on the bed. He kissed her neck and the hollow between her breasts. He worked his way around and removed her bra, and she enjoyed every moment. Nate's hands and his mouth were everywhere. She realized their pants were gone when she heard the crucial rip of packaging that meant he knew they needed to be safe. They stared at each other and kissed again. There was a new sensation of his firm flesh, she wanted to feel it over and over again, and for it never to stop as he made love to her. It was deep, slow, and they both met an apex together.

Amina had imagined sex with him would be good, but she never dreamed it would be this good. Nate wrapped Amina in his arms, tight and secure.

He kissed her shoulder, neck, her ear. "Are you okay?" he whispered.

She intertwined her hands in his and inched closer to him. "I'm fine."

"Good."

"Nate, at some point, you'll need to go to my car and grab my bag." Amina was thrilled to be wrapped up with him.

"Was this all a part of some devious, sinister plan to come to my home and take me to bed with you?"

"I just try to be prepared." She laughed.

He pulled her closer and inhaled deeply. "Good night," he whispered.

Amina drifted off, a smile planted on her face.

Chapter Eight

THE NEXT MORNING Nate snuck a peek at Amina upstairs in the bedroom. She stood in her towel, and he thought of them together last night, how good her body felt against his. He climbed the stairs to meet her, and when he reached the top step, her towel hit the floor.

"What was taking you so long?" She stood naked in front of him, ready for more.

Nate rushed over and kissed her and placed her on the bed. She climbed on top of him. He lay on his back, and she shook her hand in his face to signal for protection. He was quick and provided what was needed. He moved her hips around him, and she bit her lip. He kissed her breasts and massaged them, and she ran her fingers through his hair. They made love that morning as sunlight filled his loft.

Amina lay with her head on his chest as he trailed his fingertips along her back.

"What time do you start today?" she whispered.

"Eight, so we'll have to start getting ready soon."

"We have to leave our bubble and start the day, officially

this time." She smiled at him.

They both climbed out of bed and got ready.

"Do you have everything?" he asked while he walked her to her car with her hand in his.

"Yes, thanks. I'm going to be in meetings all day, and I won't be getting home until later. I'll call you when I get home. Thanks for grabbing my stuff from the car."

"Not a problem. Are you sure you'll be able to make it through the day without me?" Nate swung Amina to face him. He shot her a sexy grin.

"It'll be hard, but I'm gonna do my best." She reached up, kissed his cheek, and bit his earlobe, and he laughed.

He put her bag in the back of her SUV, and walked her to the driver's side of her car.

"Oh, it's Thursday. Tonight is like family night. Angela comes over with David, and we all have dinner together. If you're free, you can come over. It will be around seven."

"Are you sure that's okay?"

"Yeah, it's fine." Amina pulled him close, while her back was pressed against the car door.

"Okay, yeah, I'll have to come home and change first, but I'll come." He pressed his body against hers.

He put his hand on her face and smiled. She put her hands on his face, and rubbed his beard.

When Nate arrived at the hospital, he whistled one of his favorite songs while he waited in line for his coffee. He continued whistling as he walked the corridors to his office, as he waved good morning to various hospital staff. There was a huge weight lifted off of him. For the last two years, he'd thought something was wrong with him. He felt like he wasn't good enough for any woman. That he needed to change who he was as a person. That he needed to be who Shawn wanted him to be or be unambitious like Stacy wanted. For the first time in a long time, he felt great just being him, and being him seemed to be enough. At least it was enough for Amina, and that was all that mattered.

Shawn greeted him as he made it to his office. "Hey, man, what's up? How are you?"

"I'm good. How did everything go last night? Dr. Heller ended up being on call, sorry. I know we usually do our on calls together, but they told me that he took it over for some reason."

"He had a patient that had an intense surgery earlier in the day, and he didn't want to leave the hospital. He stayed around, said he would cover on-call duties, which worked out."

"Thanks, man. I told Amina a little bit more about being on the surgery team this morning." He immediately regretted that slipped out.

"Wait, back up." Shawn motioned his hands backward, with a huge smile on his face. "This morning?" Thankfully they were inside of Nate's office, and he closed the door.

"Okay, very quickly, I will fill you in, and then I have to go check on patients. Okay?"

"Well, break it down." Shawn smiled.

"Amina came over for dinner last night, and well, she left this morning." He couldn't help it. He smiled at the memory of their night and morning together.

"What!" Shawn yelled. "Wow, I'm happy for you. Not because you got some action."

Nate sighed. It was far from action.

"I'm happy because you seem happy, so far anyway. I honestly didn't think you had in you. I didn't think you would know what to do with all of that."

Nate grinned. He knew exactly what to do. He did it well and couldn't wait to do it again and again.

"We'll have to talk more about this later."

"Sounds good."

Shawn walked out of Nate's office, and his phone vibrated in his pocket.

Thank you for last night, and this morning. Better than I could have ever imagined. And thank Shawn for bringing you to the gala. I think we owe him. UGH! I hope you have a good day. Is it bad I miss you? See you soon

I miss you too, so it's not bad, not bad at all. And yes, we owe Shawn. Looking forward to seeing you soon.

Oh, last night and this morning INCREDIBLE!

He made his rounds, followed up with patients, and reviewed files on others. Then he finally made it to Ryan; he needed to monitor her pain.

"Hey, you're Dr. Moore, right?" Ryan smiled.

"Yes, I just got added to your surgery team with Dr. Atkins. How are we feeling today?" He smiled and gave her a fist bump.

"Today is a good one. The Warriors play a preseason game tonight, and it's a national game so I can watch."

He grinned. "Hi, Mr. and Mrs. Harris. How did everything go last night?"

"She had a good night. Dr. Heller said that the scans should be back today to see if the tumor has gotten any smaller."

"Yes, Dr. Heller is right. Those should be coming in today, and they'll take a look at them and take it from there. How's the pain, Ryan?"

"Not too bad, much better than it was about a week ago."

"Oh, that's really good. A positive sign. Did you guys have any other questions before I go?"

"Just keep us posted on those scan results," Mr. Harris said.

Nate fist-bumped Ryan goodbye, then went home, showered, changed, and set out for Amina's.

He was a block away when he saw two police cars. The scene looked so out of place on this quiet tree-lined street. Amina's car was in the driveway, and a police car was parked behind it. His heart raced. He parked at least two blocks away and walked down to her house. Angela was outside and gave the okay for him to be waved through. She looked

IESHIA WIEDLIN

shaken to her core.

"Hey, Angela, how are you? What's going on? Is Amina okay?" he asked.

Was it a robbery or violent attack?

"Hey, Nate. Well, luckily, she has the Ring and cameras all around her house. So glad she listened to her dad about that, especially living by herself. Someone—well, not someone, her ex, Omar, tried to break into her house either last night or early this morning. By looking at your face, she hasn't filled you in on him yet." He shook his head. "Well, apparently, based on talking to some of the neighbors, he's been watching her comings and goings, and she has a restraining order on him." Angela's voice rose.

"Are you serious?" He couldn't believe what he heard. "Where's Amina now? Is she okay?"

"She's fine. I mean, not fine, she's a bit shaken up. Of course, she's wondering what would've happened if she were home." Angela was stressed and overwhelmed.

He just wanted to hold Amina. Nate looked around every tree, every corner, every bush, and he wondered. Had Omar watched them when they walked to dinner, to the bakery? Who was this guy? He needed answers.

"Nate, did you want to go inside?" Angela broke into his stream of thoughts.

"Yes, sure, of course."

They walked inside and over to the couch into the living room.

"This is David," Angela introduced him to Nate.

"Hey, David, nice to meet you." He was a handsome kid, looked a lot like his mom, with his caramel skin and big brown eyes.

"Hello, Dr. Moore." Nate smiled.

"You can call me Nate."

"Okay. Auntie Mina is in her office."

"Thanks, dude." He looked at Angela for the okay to go inside, and she motioned with her head toward the hall.

He walked into Amina's office and leaned against the doorframe. She looked up from her desk.

"Hey, Nate." Her voice broke.

He walked over and enveloped her in his arms. He held her as tightly as he could, until she was ready to let go.

"I'm sorry, Nate."

He stroked his thumb across her face. "Please never apologize to me for being angry or upset over something so frightening. I'm glad I'm here."

"I didn't want to have the conversation about my ex, Omar, like this. I knew it was something we needed to talk about. It just never seemed like the right time, you know?"

"I know, and we'll talk about all of that, just not at this moment. I just want to know you're okay." He walked her over to the couch in her office and sat her down.

"I mean, I'm sort of okay. My mind just keeps wondering what the goal was if I had been here."

Nate held her hand and rubbed her back. "Angela said

the neighbors mentioned something about him watching you."

Amina nodded. She put her head on his shoulder, and he continued to hold her hand.

David walked in. He asked Amina when they were going to eat.

She smiled at him. "I'll be in there in a minute, sweetheart."

"Okay, Auntie."

"I'm just glad that you're okay. I'm glad I'm here, and you're not going through this all alone."

"Me too." Amina stood up and pulled Nate from the couch.

"Is pizza okay for dinner? With everything that's happened, I'm not in the mood to cook anything."

"Sounds perfect."

When the pizza arrived, they all sat down at the dining room table. David asked Nate lots of questions about being a doctor, and probably about a million questions about *Star Wars* once he knew that Nate loved it too. Angela didn't pry at dinner, but her worried face was hard to hide every time she looked at her friend. David helped Amina clear the table, and Nate got a glimpse into their relationship when he walked by the kitchen. Amina sat at the bar and talked to David about school and girls he had his eyes on. She tried to smile while she listened, but it didn't touch her eyes.

"Thanks for helping me out, bud."

"No problem, Auntie, happy I could help."

Angela startled Nate in the hallway. "Hey, you're staying with her tonight, right? If not, David and I could stay."

"Yeah, I planned on staying. Pretty sure I have some clothes in my car, but no way am I leaving her alone."

"Good." She hugged him.

After David finished helping Amina clean up the kitchen, it was time for them to leave.

"Do you mind walking them to their car?" Amina asked Nate.

"Sure, I have to move my car anyway. No problem." He kissed her, grabbed his jacket, and walked them outside.

When he got to his car, he opened his trunk to make sure he still had a couple of his bags there. He usually tried to keep a few changes of clothes in case he went to the gym or if he had to stay overnight at the hospital.

The more he thought about this guy hurting Amina, the more he wanted to kick his ass. He gripped the bag he found tightly and imagined it was Omar's neck. He'd only known her for a short time, but he'd seen how important she was to so many people. Was Omar watching her right now while she stood on the front porch and waited on Nate to move his car? Should he ask her to stay with him at the loft? Was it right for him to be thinking this way? He took a deep breath and tried to calm himself down. He grabbed his bags and moved his car into her driveway.

"What was taking you so long? I got cold so I came back

inside," Amina said.

"Sorry about that. I was looking to see if I had some bags in the trunk of my car."

"Bags?" Amina came around the corner from the living room.

"I didn't want you to be here alone. I want to stay here with you tonight if that's okay?" Nerves filled every word.

"You know what"—she moved closer to him—"I'm happy you asked. I was anticipating staying up all night because I was afraid to sleep. But at least if I can't sleep, I'll have someone to keep me company."

He hugged her. "Is there anything you need me to do?"

"No, me and David took care of everything."

It was late, and they both had to get up early in the morning for work, but they needed to lock up the house. They locked all the doors, all the windows, and double-checked them before heading upstairs to her bedroom.

Chapter Nine

AMINA LAY WITH her head planted against Nate's chest. She thought having him beside her would make it easier to sleep, but she was wide awake. She felt his fingertips against her arm.

"Still awake?" he whispered.

"Yeah, can't sleep."

"Me either."

After a few minutes, he said, "So, can I ask what happened with this guy? I mean, I understand if you don't want to talk about it, but if you need to talk about it, I'm here. I'm here to listen if you need to talk," he rambled.

"Nate, it's fine. I don't have a problem talking about it."

"Are you sure?"

She sat up, leaned over and kissed him, and crossed her legs. "It is okay. It's a little similar to your story. We met as first-year students in college. Coming out of high school, I didn't date a lot, didn't have a long-term boyfriend or anything like that. So the thought of having a long-term relationship or dating in college was something I was very open to, but it was also a whole new world to me.

"Anyway, Omar and I had a class together. He was cute, tall, sweet smile, kind. We saw each other, liked each other, he asked me out, and we became excellent friends and then became closer than friends. For some reason, Angela always said there was something about him she just didn't like, just a vibe she got. She put up with him though because I liked him. We were roommates in college, you know. Did I ever tell you that?"

Nate shook his head.

"So anyway, we dated the rest of college and didn't have any major issues. We had an excellent, healthy, loving, fun relationship. We went to a ton of football games, dinners, movies, everything was good. The problems started once we graduated. I found a job straightaway, working for a non-profit in Detroit. Me and Angela moved into the city because she got a job there as well. He stayed in Ann Arbor because he wanted to go to law school since he couldn't find work, which was cool. After all, it was only a forty-five-minute drive, so no problem. Anytime plans changed or I was late, he accused me of cheating."

"Are you serious?" Nate asked. "It sounds like you never gave him a reason to think that at all."

"Yeah, every single time. We had this major fight, and we broke up; he just snapped. That was the first time he raised his voice at me, and I didn't know how to respond. It was like the person that I first met in college just wasn't there.

"Angela ended up meeting this guy, Kevin. She was head over heels and moved in with him. They got married a few years down the line. I miss him. Anyway, Omar eventually came back and apologized, and he seemed like himself, like the Omar I fell in love with. We talked, and things seemed good, then he moved in with me.

"It started with him criticizing my clothes. He had a problem with everything I wore to work, to school when I started going for my master's—wherever, it was an issue. Then, it was emotional and verbal abuse. And then, yes, he started hitting me. He did it once, and I left. I stayed with Angela for about a week or so, and she and Kevin were ready to go and kill him. I'm honestly not sure how they didn't. I went back home to pack some more clothes, and Omar and I talked. We ended up getting back together." She sighed, ashamed of her choices.

Nate's hands twisted around the blankets.

"It was better. Omar was working, and we were going on double dates with Angela and Kev. Omar felt horrible for what he had done and how he acted. It was all good. My brother would come and hang out with us, and they ended up becoming very close over time. Omar promised that he would never hurt me or hit me ever again.

"Then he lost his job, and the abuse came back with a vengeance. This time, though, my brother became his advocate. I told him about what was going on because I didn't want my dad to know. Amir thought maybe Omar was sick, like he was having a mental break or something. He couldn't imagine Omar doing something like that to me. He was making excuses for him, you know? He was saying I shouldn't leave him, that I should be trying to get him help and work things out with him. That Omar didn't need me kicking him while he was down."

"What a bunch of bullshit! That is the most idiotic thing I have ever heard! Why wouldn't he be concerned about you being safe?!" he shouted.

She placed her hand on his arm and glanced at him.

"Sorry to yell. I just can't believe this. It's all so awful."

"I know. To make this awful story shorter, because I don't want to get into the long version, Omar beat me up pretty badly and tried to rape me. I called Angela after he left our apartment for the day. She took me to the emergency room. I made a police report and got a restraining order right away.

"We called Amir and made him come to the hospital to see what Omar did, and he kept with his same routine of something might be wrong with him. I got fired from like three jobs because Omar kept trying to come to my jobs or I kept missing work afraid he would come to my jobs. I talked to my dad and decided to move back to Chicago. I finally had to tell him about everything that was going on. He told me he knew something was up. I never sounded right, but he had to wait for me to be honest with him. He trusted me to work through it and to figure things out in my way. When I told him, though, he was angry and sad for me that I went through something so awful, even though he was so happy I was coming back home.

"When I went back to Michigan for Angie and Kevin's wedding, I was terrified Omar was going to find out about it somehow and show up out of nowhere. But if he did, there were some good men there fully prepared. Some of them wanted him to. That pretty much leads us to today. I got a restraining order put in place when I moved here. We also have one for my dad, Angela, and David. Amir didn't want to get one because he stood by his feelings on Omar. They had gotten so close, and Omar didn't have the best relationship with his family. Amir couldn't bring himself to turn his back on him despite everything that Omar did to me. That's pretty much where we are, and everything awful that happened between us. It all just came crashing back down tonight and started hitting me all at once."

She was exhausted.

Nate reached out, hugged her. "I'm so sorry. Sorry for all the hurt and pain you went through."

"I know, and I appreciate that. I try very hard not to overthink it. The police are involved, and they have to do their job. I have the cameras at my house because of Omar's craziness." She picked at a thread on her duvet cover, afraid to meet Nate's eyes. "I appreciate you not running from my house, screaming. I have been dreading telling you any of this. I didn't know how you would respond. It's all a lot. I know that, so I understand if you decide to leave quietly in the morning. I was dating a guy a bit after all of this with Omar. I told him all of this, and I never saw him again. I get it. So thanks for at least staying the night." She gave him a small smile when her eyes met his.

He stared at her.

"Are you okay?" she asked.

"Yeah, I'm okay, just sad that you had to go through all of that." Nate shrugged.

Amina leaned over and gave him a small, sweet kiss on the lips. "Thank you for listening and being here tonight. I don't want to talk about this anymore, okay?" She tried to memorize his face. He would be gone when morning came.

"Got it. That reminds me." He grinned and grabbed the TV remote that sat on the stand next to her bed. "There's a Warriors preseason game on tonight, and I have a patient I need to talk to about this tomorrow."

"Yes, that would be much better than talking about this." She rested comfortably in Nate's arms as they watched the game. She listened to his breathing, and it sang her gently to sleep.

Chapter Ten

NATE WOKE UP the next morning a bit disoriented. He sat up, looked at the other side of the bed, and realized he'd slept at Amina's. All of yesterday's events roared back. He never would have imagined that the night would've ended the way it did, considering how the day started. He looked at her side of the bed again. Where was she?

He smelled the coffee coming from the kitchen and heard slow, moody music playing. He was unsettled, still processing everything Amina shared with him last night. Sure, Amina was beautiful, and kind, but he didn't want to put her life in jeopardy. Had Omar seen them together and that sent him into a rage? The last thing Nate wanted was to bring more harm into her life. He didn't want to give Omar any more ammunition, but he didn't want to walk away from her either. He sighed, walked over to the bathroom, splashed some cold water on his face, brushed his teeth, and went downstairs.

He saw Amina from the hallway. She sat in her robe, hair up in a bun. She stared at her laptop, coffee in hand, and sang along to whatever song was playing. He wasn't sure how she could look like this first thing in the morning, especially after everything that happened last night. She seemed so calm, not at all afraid of everything she shared with him yesterday. He would be a fool to not give things a chance with this woman who was so strong and made him laugh like no one else. Why should he give up one of the best things that happened to him in a long time? Running away would be so final, and they had time to see what happened next. He shook his head and walked into the kitchen.

"Hey, good morning!" Amina said.

"Good morning." He kissed her on the cheek.

There were so many things he wanted to do with her, but he settled on this.

"I made coffee. I wasn't exactly sure what you wanted to eat for breakfast, but I can make something for you if you want."

"Um, do you have any bagels? I don't usually eat a heavy breakfast in the morning, so you don't need to fix me anything." He sat down next to her at the kitchen bar.

"I don't mind."

"It's fine." He smiled.

"Well, mugs are over there, bagels are there, cream cheese in the fridge." Amina smiled as she pointed everything out to him. "What time do you have to be at the hospital?"

"I don't see my first patient until a little after nine, so no rush this morning. What about you? Are you going into the office this morning?"

"Well, I emailed my director this morning. He's always up very early like me. I told him about everything that happened yesterday, and he told me that I could take the day off. It's Friday, and we typically don't have meetings on Fridays. So, I'm probably just going to hang out here today."

He sat down next to her with his bagel and coffee. "What's this song playing? I remember it from Sunday."

"'Real Love Baby' by Father John Misty. It's good, right?" She grinned.

"Yeah, pretty good. I mean, I never heard of him before, but it sounds all right."

She smiled. "Not the first time I've heard that. I drive Angela and Amir up the wall with my music." She laughed. "They refer to everything I listen to as my whiny music. When we were in college, she would get annoyed with me, called me a music snob all the time. I make playlists for her, and I know she never listens to them, but whatever. Same with Amir and me. We sort of agree on hip-hop, strictly nineties. Aside from that, he hates anything I share with him too." She snickered.

"I'm partial to early 2000s hip-hop myself." He straightened up next to her.

"Nice. I make playlists all the time. I've become a total weirdo about it."

"My parents listened to a lot of R & B and soul music when I was growing up. It stuck. I tend to listen to that a lot.

I was like a huge Usher fan when I was younger."

Amina flung her head back as she laughed. "The sight of you singing along to Usher is one I need to see."

"Anyway"—he laughed—"I can find these playlists?"

"Yep, just search me on Spotify."

"I most certainly will. How did you and Angela become such good friends?"

"Oh, well, Angie and I met in high school. I was shy, and she wasn't. In tenth grade, we were paired for a project in science class. At the time, she was going out with this guy named Matt, a top-rated football player at school. Everybody loved Matt; everyone did not love Angela going out with him. Anyway, one day, three girls…one of them liked Matt and hated he was so into Angela."

Nate nodded as he listened. How could she be like this so early? She was animated with her hands as she talked to him, so filled with life.

"We were in class, going over our project, and this girl walked by and started making monkey sounds."

"Oh, hell no!" Nate shouted.

"Yes, she did. Then her friends were like gassing her up to do it more and to say something to Angela. At that point, she grabbed my hand because she didn't want to haul off and hit this girl. So this dumb girl comes up and says, 'You know the only reason he's not with me is that I don't give it up like you.' I was so pissed. So I got up and got in this girl's face and said, 'No, you stupid shit, he's not with you because

you're ugly as hell,' and punched her. The rest is history."
Amina laughed. "I broke my hand but gained a lifelong
friend."

"So, I was right to step in that night we met?"

"I had a reason to be worried about breaking my hand."

"Last night, you said you missed Kevin. What happened?" He tried to be gentle with his question.

Amina sighed, and her whole demeanor changed. "Kevin
died in a car accident when David was five. It was heartbreaking. He was such a good man to Angie and a
phenomenal father to D. He was the best. I'm sure the two
of you would have been fast friends." She leaned into him.

"Oh, I'm sorry."

"It's okay, it's been years, but it's still sad. David looks
like his mom, but the way he cares for his mom, how he
helps her and wants to be his best for her—that's totally
Kevin." She smiled. "So the gala night is our night, that's her
free-pass night, and she lives it up."

Nate nodded. He was reminded of something he was
supposed to ask her before all the craziness of last night.

"What's the look for?"

"Well, I have something to ask you, and I know it's short
notice. I understand if you say no or you can't make it." She
motioned for him to keep going. "On Saturday, there's an
event honoring African-American doctors. I've been going
for the last couple of years." He immediately put a finger up
and stopped Amina from whatever it was she was about to

say, and they laughed. "I've worked with a few doctors who have been honored. On Saturday, they are honoring Shawn." Nate put up his finger again. "I wanted to know if you would go with me."

"People are going to acknowledge Shawn publicly?" Amina snickered.

"I know, crazy, right?" he said. "Despite all of his nonsense, he's a great surgeon. It's well deserved, and please never tell him I said that," he joked.

"What time is the event?"

"Let me go grab my phone. I have it in an email. Cocktail hour is at four, then it's a dinner, and the ceremony honoring some designated guests. Oh, and it's black-tie."

"So, let me get this straight, black-tie tomorrow afternoon?"

"I figured since you've had these last few years working on the galas, you might have a dress or two for the occasion. Did you have something going on tomorrow?" he asked.

"Lucky for you, no, because Michigan plays a night game and my dad and I don't get together for those. But that's not the point." She elbowed him. "Let me just check with Angie to see if she can come over and do my makeup. She's so much better than I am at that kind of stuff."

"Could she come to my place?" He smiled. "I also wanted to know if you can stay at my place tonight."

"Why are you asking me that?" Amina blinked, confused.

"Well, I'm not sure how comfortable you feel about being here all day alone after everything that happened yesterday, and it would make things easier for tomorrow." Her calm appearance made him feel better; the fact she wasn't panicked was a good sign. She was so brave when she shared everything with him last night; he needed to be bold and clear about what he wanted.

"Let me text Angie. She's up right now."

Nate circled his fingers around his coffee cup, and shook his foot on the barstool as he awaited her response while she texted back and forth with Angela. He could only imagine what was happening with this conversation between the two of them.

"She said yes. So, let me go see what I can pull together for this event tomorrow."

"Wait, so…" He was so anxious he didn't understand what she said.

"Yes, Nate. Yes, to all of it. How much time do I have before you leave for work?"

He was thrilled. "It's seven now. About an hour."

Amina grinned. "An hour to pack for the weekend and pull together a black-tie event outfit, no big deal." She shrugged as she walked upstairs.

He finished his coffee and bagel and made his way upstairs and found her frantic as she moved around in her bedroom. Clothes and shoes were everywhere. She apparently didn't realize he'd entered the room. He grabbed his bag and went into the bathroom to shower and get himself together for the day. By the time he came out, things were much calmer in the room.

"How does this look?" She pointed to the dress she laid out on the bed. A wine-colored halter dress that would look exquisite against her skin.

He grinned as he looked at it and pulled her to his side. "I hate I have to be at work. I would love nothing more than to make love to you right now." He kissed her and ran his hands over her body.

"That is indeed a shame because I would love nothing more," she whispered.

She pulled away from him.

"Do you mind waiting for me downstairs? I'll call you up when I'm done, and you can carry everything down and to the car."

He nodded slowly. She kissed him and sent him away, or they would've never left the house.

Chapter Eleven

AMINA GOT A call from her brother to meet him for lunch. He wasn't too far away from Nate's place, so she decided to meet him. She texted Nate to let him know as well.

When she arrived at the bar to meet Amir, she started to feel uncomfortable. She was out in the open, exposed. What if Omar were watching, what if he followed them, what if he was here? Her phone rang, and she jumped.

"Hello?"

"Hey. It's me, are you okay?"

She smiled at the sound of his voice. So calm and gentle.

"Hey, Nate. I'm okay, just waiting on Amir at this bar. A little nervous being out here, you know?"

"Of course you are. That makes total sense. I can talk to you for a bit until he gets there. I read somewhere that if a woman is on the phone, sometimes it can deter a creeper from approaching them."

"Nate, what the hell are you reading these days?"

He laughed.

"I got here, sat down, and immediately wanted to leave. I haven't felt that way in a while. All this stuff with Omar is just stirring up a lot of uneasiness I thought I was done dealing with."

"I'm sorry this is happening to you. Will Amir be there soon?"

At that precise moment, Amir walked through the door and waved.

"He just got here, so I have to go. Thanks for calling to check on me."

"Anytime. Eat light, dinner tonight."

She pictured that sexy grin of his. Even streets away, he affected her body.

"Will do. See you soon."

"What's up?" Amir hugged her. "Who were you talking to that's getting you to smile like that? Was it the doctor?"

"I am not answering that." She laughed with her brother while they grabbed a table.

"I got your text last night about Omar. Sorry I didn't get back to you."

Amina didn't say anything. She wasn't sure how this conversation was going to go. Any discussion about Omar could go off the rails pretty quickly.

"Yeah, I came home, and the back window was broken. I called the police, and we looked at the security cameras, and there he was, as clear as day. Angela talked to a few of my neighbors, and he's been around the house for a while now."

"Are you sure it wasn't a mistake?" Amir asked as he took his beer from the waiter.

"Mir, how would that be a mistake? I know how Omar looks. We dated for four years. Why are you always so quick to defend him? After everything he has done, all of the hurt and the damage he has done to me, you are still sitting here defending him. I mean, what the hell?"

"I'm not defending him. I just wonder, you know, maybe if you just talk to him—"

"Stop!" She cut him off. "Why would I talk to him, Mir? Why? Why did you want to meet me today? You could've done this shit over the phone. I came here to spend time with you, not to be hassled about Omar's crazy ass."

Amir took a deep breath. "I don't mean to make you feel bad. I'm trying to see if there's a way to deal with him without having the police involved. I mean, I know after everything he did I haven't been around the way I should have. I'm just trying to do right by you both."

"Do you realize how stupid you sound? I'm your sister! You should be more concerned about me, not him! It's always about him. How it was a bad look for him to be arrested. Or a bad look for him to have abuse charges. You never thought about how any of that was affecting me. Do you know how much that hurt me?" She fought her tears. "Like, what do you want me to do?" She threw her hands up, so disappointed that he wouldn't let his defense of Omar go.

"Mina, I'm sorry I wasn't there for you when Omar was

abusing you the way he was. I'm sorry that you went through that. But—"

Amina slammed her hand on the table. "The fact you are saying *but* at the end of that sentence means you don't mean a word of what you're saying. Deep down, you are still trying to defend him. I can't sit here and listen to any more of this bullshit!" Her voice broke with every word she spoke, but she didn't want her tears to fall in front of Amir.

She grabbed her stuff and left her brother sitting at the table. She called Angela when she got outside.

"Mina, try to calm down. Where are you going?" Angela asked.

"Back to Nate's."

"Okay, get there, and try to relax. Take a hot shower and try to shake the day off. When is Nate coming home?"

"He said around 4:30. I have to try to get myself together before then." She sighed.

"Mina, I know you're pissed. I'm pissed for you. Just try to calm down."

They talked until she got back to the loft, and she followed Angela's advice. She took a long, hot shower. She slid into a pair of black jeans and a long-sleeve T-shirt and sat on his massive couch until he got home.

AMINA WAS CURLED up on the couch, with ESPN on, her laptop next to her, and she was asleep. She felt the scruff of his beard and the softness of his lips as he kissed her cheek. She smiled as she opened her eyes.

"Hey, Nate." Her voice was full of sleep.

"I got your text that you got home. Thanks for letting me know. It was quick. What happened?" he asked.

"You want to talk about it now, or do you want to wait until dinner?"

"That bad, huh?" He placed his hand on her face and stroked her cheek.

Amina didn't want to go to dinner. She would've sat on the couch and kissed him all night.

"It was awful."

"Well, let's talk about it over dinner. What are you in the mood for?"

"Pizza. I'm so hungry right now," she said.

"Okay, let me change. Give me about fifteen minutes, and we can be on our way."

They walked hand in hand into the chilly October Chicago night to grab some pizza. Amina felt the eyes of every group of young ladies that passed. She wasn't sure if it was because of how hot Nate looked or the fact that he was holding her hand. She tried to ignore them, but every eye was focused on them, and the fact she was Black was a glaring white hot light on them. This was what she was afraid of, all of the eyes following every move they made.

They walked into the restaurant, and it was busy as expected for a Friday night. Despite the crowd being pretty diverse, more eyes greeted them. This time they were followed by whispers. Amina dropped his hand when an older African-American couple stared at them. She felt ashamed, and like she was letting them down. She noticed one of the players hiding out in the corner of the waiting room as well. His faced was shocked when they walked in. Amina saw him lean down to whisper to whoever his date was as Nate guided Amina to a seat in the waiting area.

He kissed her on the cheek. She felt his long eyelashes and his beard against her skin; she tried to pull away quickly, but it was like he lit a match on her body.

"I'm going to see how long the wait is, okay?" he whispered.

"I'll wait here." Her eyes followed him.

She couldn't bear to look around the room, to take in how many continued to stare at them.

Nate came back about five minutes later. "It's going to be about fifteen to twenty minutes," he said and sat down next to her.

While they sat and waited, the door opened, and Nate's friend Chris and his wife walked in. Amina was happy to have a welcome distraction while they waited.

"Hey! Nate, Amina, how are you guys?"

"Oh, hey, Chris, what's up? How are you doing, man?"

"I'm doing well. I haven't seen you at the gym in the last couple of days. Everything okay?"

"Yes, everything is fine. Just been a little busy."

"You remember my wife, Gabriella."

"Yes, I do."

Amina sat and waited for Nate to introduce her and she was speechless when he didn't. She stood and introduced herself to Chris's wife while Nate stood lost in his thoughts. All of her worries about dating a white man were being realized. He was afraid or embarrassed to introduce her to people amid all the uncomfortable stares and whispers.

"All right, well, we're going to head over to the bar. Nice seeing you again, Amina; hope to see you at the gym soon, Nate."

"Okay, Chris, good to see you guys."

"Table for Dr. Moore." Nate reached for her hand, and she didn't take it.

Amina was fuming as she walked to the table with Nate behind her. She sat down across from him and couldn't bear to look at him.

"Did you want to talk about your lunch with Amir?" He adjusted himself in his seat and tried to get comfortable.

She sighed. "No. I want to know why you are incapable of introducing me to someone. Why was that so difficult? Do you not want people to know that you're seeing a Black woman? All the stares and whispers too much for you?" Amina's voice started to rise.

"Now you know that's ridiculous. I'm not embarrassed by you, Amina, or by the fact that you're Black. I couldn't give two shits about anybody's stares."

"Then why not introduce to me Chris's wife?"

"I didn't know how to introduce you. I didn't know what to call you."

Her hands dropped to her lap, and she stared at him. "What to call me? I thought I was your friend. I mean, you could've at least called me your friend."

"I don't make love to my friends."

Amina didn't take the compliment, and she didn't like his tone. He spoke to her like she did something wrong.

"So, we're not friends—are we sex buddies? I mean, we're not in a relationship because I would think you would want to be friends with that person. And be proud to introduce them to people. I guess that's not the case here."

The waitress came back, he ordered a pizza, and asked for it to go. The only thing Amina said to him was what she wanted on her pizza. She texted Angela to let her know this was a huge mistake. They sat in silence, not looking at each other until the pizza came for them to take home. They walked back to Nate's without uttering a word to one another.

Once they got back to the loft, Amina went straight upstairs and changed out of her clothes. When she came back down, still pretty upset, a singer's voice filled his loft to break a bit of the tension. She sat at the table, poured herself a glass of wine, put pizza on her plate, and sighed as she looked across the table at him.

"What happened tonight?" she finally asked.

He sat across the table and sipped his wine. "I'm sorry I didn't introduce you to Chris's wife. The thing is, Amina, I freaked out a little bit."

She snorted. "Why? Introducing me to someone causes you to freak out?"

"No, that's not why I was freaking out. I was freaking out because I didn't want to say the wrong thing. I didn't want to say *friend* because, yes, you are my friend, but you seem more to me than that. I didn't want to say *girlfriend* because that seemed presumptuous, and I didn't want to put a label on something that we haven't talked about. Why did you automatically assume it was about you being Black?"

"Did you not see all the eyes on us tonight? Did you miss the pointing of the fingers and whispers? I guess it seemed too much. It felt like it was too much for me. This is all so new to me."

"Amina, you have to stop worrying about what other people think. I don't care at all what they think. It's not that big of a deal."

"Maybe not to you, but it is for me."

"Why? Why does it matter how other people think and feel about seeing us together?"

Amina sat quietly as she tried to figure out the words to explain why it was a big deal. She had this idea in her mind of who she would end up with, and none of those men looked like Nate. She couldn't figure out how to explain any of that to him.

He pushed away from the table and walked over to her. He took her hands, stood her up, and looked her in the eyes with his hand on her face. "I want you to know that you can talk to me about anything. If you have some feelings about being with me or you're worried about us being out together, you can't be afraid of talking to me. Okay?"

Amina nodded, her hands pressed into his strong chest, and stared into his blue eyes.

He stroked his thumb against her cheek. "Amina, if we're gonna be together, please be honest with me, that's all I ask. But please understand, none of what happened tonight was about you being Black. I just didn't want to say the wrong thing. So far, things have been so great, and I didn't want to say anything to screw it all up. I—"

She kissed him while he was in midsentence. Slow and gentle, they kissed each other.

"Make love to me," she whispered against his lips.

Nate's breath caught, and all the slow and gentle kisses were gone. He kissed Amina hard. She broke away from him, grabbed his hand, and led him upstairs.

She stood in front of him at the foot of his massive bed. "I'm sorry for being angry with you at dinner and assuming the worst." She took off his shirt, put her hands on his chest, and smiled up at him.

He put his hand against her cheek and kissed her. "I'm sorry, too, but I still don't know what to call you." He laughed.

"Well, what do you want to call me?"

"Can we talk about it later?" he asked with a grin.

"Yes."

Amina's body was filled with anticipation as he lifted her shirt over her head, along with her bra. Nate kissed every part of her he could reach while she stood in front of him. Amina moaned with enjoyment as he found more places he could kiss. Amina giggled when he lifted her up, laid her on the bed, and removed the rest of her pajamas. Then he made love to her, just like she asked.

Chapter Twelve

NATE GENTLY GUIDED Amina from bed. They climbed downstairs and finished dinner, and kissed each other as they cleaned up the kitchen and put away the leftover pizza. He still had a little bit of wine to finish; she stood and stared at him while he chugged the rest down. She stepped over to him, tugged on his boxer briefs, and kissed him. She wanted more. Like him in the kitchen with nothing else on. She couldn't control herself. He kissed her back, picked her up, and set her on top of the island. He opened her robe slightly, and they made love right there.

Amina woke up in the middle of the night, and it took her minute to get her bearings. She realized she was at Nate's loft, and he was asleep next to her. She tried to be as quiet as possible, making a quick trip to the bathroom and getting back to bed, but she woke him up.

"Everything okay?" His voice was so husky and sexy in the middle of the night. He rolled over and gazed up at her and moved her hair away from her face.

"Yes, everything's fine." Even in the dark room, she saw

how handsome he was.

He put his hand on her face. "You're so beautiful."

She leaned down and kissed him.

She lay down next to him and put her head on his chest and interlaced her fingers in his. "You never answered my question, you know. And we should probably be clear on this, considering we have an event this evening where you're going to be introducing to me to a lot of doctors."

Nate's body moved as he laughed. "Well"—he pulled her closer—"I would like you to be my girlfriend. I know it's a silly thing, but I want to be in a relationship with you. I care about you, and I don't want to see anyone else but you. I enjoy being with you, and I would like for us to be together. If that's okay with you."

She smiled. He was someone she could trust and confide in, someone she knew would be there for her. She sat up and stared at him. Being with him was something brand new, and Amina knew he would help guide her through it all. Nate put his hand on her face, and the way he kissed her made her body yearn for him.

"I would like that. I would like it very much." She kissed him again, climbed on top of him, and showed him how much she liked it.

She woke up in the morning, reached out for him, and found only a piece of paper.

AMINA,

I DIDN'T WANT TO WAKE YOU UP. YOU LOOK SO

BEAUTIFUL EVEN WHEN YOU'RE ASLEEP. ANYWAY, I HAD SOME ERRANDS TO RUN. I SHOULD BE BACK HOME IN A COUPLE OF HOURS. SEE YOU SOON. LAST NIGHT WAS AMAZING. YOU ARE AN INCREDIBLE WOMAN.

YOURS,
NATE

Amina ran over her finger over the word *yours*. She glanced at his alarm clock and realized it was almost noon. Amina hurried out of bed because Angela would be there soon. She had to make sure her hair and makeup were right for this event. She fixed herself some coffee, grabbed something to eat, and her laptop and cell phone to check all of her missed messages.

She had a few voice mails, and one was an apology from Amir. She deleted it before she could even bring herself to listen to the rest of it. The next was from one of the officers. He let her know they might have a lead on Omar, who was spotted again near her home. It was a good thing he was still in the area—that meant the odds of him being found were greater. She was frightened, but she pushed down her fear to stay focused on her night with Nate. Everything needed to be perfect; this was their first night as an official couple.

Angela arrived and whistled when she walked into Nate's loft. "So this is how doctor living looks. Okay, Mina, okay. Not mad at you at all. I see you. It's beautiful."

Amina walked over and hugged her friend. She needed it.

"I know there's a lot of craziness going on with Amir and Omar, but we're not going to talk about any of that. I want all of the details about you and Nate. I shook my head so hard when I got your 'it's a mistake' text."

Amina laughed. She welcomed the good old-fashioned girl talk with her best friend. She couldn't wait to spill.

"First wine, and let me know where I can set up."

Amina gleefully filled her bestie in on all the details of their incredible passionate night together.

Angela took her hands off the island in the kitchen, a disgusted look on her face. "Please tell me that you cleaned and disinfected this island that all my makeup is sitting on and that I'm currently touching right now."

Amina tossed her head back as she laughed.

"So you and the good doctor just been getting it all over this loft, huh? I mean, it's like that?" Angela asked.

"Yes!" Amina giggled. "He is incredible! And that just doesn't even do him justice. But, yes, it's like that. It's been amazing. He's amazing."

Angela walked to the refrigerator. She grabbed a cucumber, a zucchini, and a banana off the self, and placed them on counter. "Okay, spill."

"Angie!" Amina yelled. "I will not. I cannot tell you that. I can't."

"Well, if he's been putting it down like that, I have to assume it's cucumber." She laughed. "What was with all the 'this was a mistake' nonsense?"

"Last night, were walking to dinner, and it felt like everybody was looking at us. It just felt like I had this white light on us because of the whole interracial thing."

"You cannot be serious. Come on, Mina! I can't believe you are saying this! All of the actors that you think are hot, and you're tripping about Nate being white. Come on, sis!"

Amina sighed. "I know. I had this idealized version of what my future would be and who it would be with. Never would I have imagined it would be with someone who looks like Nate. But he is amazing, and I have to find a way to deal with it."

"Yeah, you do. I mean, I have to say, Mina, I like him. I like him a lot; I wasn't sure about him at first. I mean, with the way you guys met at the gala and everything. I wasn't sure if he was as genuine as he seemed. But the way he stepped up after the Omar incident—he's been great. He was so good with D at such a stressful time, so calm and kind to him. You seem happy, and as long as he keeps making you smile the way you have been, I'm team Nate. So get over this race bullshit! Please!"

"Thanks, Angie. I will work a little harder on that."

"Plus, he's fine as hell." Angela elbowed her and laughed. "Well, I am all done, and I think I've outdone myself. I left the lip blank until I see the dress color."

Angela was finishing her makeup when Nate walked through the door.

"Hey, Angela, how are you? It's so good to see you.

Thanks so much for coming over helping Amina out." He walked over and hugged her.

Amina appreciated that he respected her best friend like that.

"No problem. Always here to help my girl out. You have such a great place, Doc."

"Thanks."

"So, where is this thing tonight?" Angela asked.

"It's over at the W hotel, in one of their ballrooms, so not too far from here, which is good. Not really up for a long drive tonight."

His hair was a little shorter and his beard was impeccable around his plump red lips. Thank goodness they were dealing with a time deadline.

"Like the haircut." Amina winked at him.

He blushed. "Thanks. Well, if you ladies would excuse me, I have to start figuring out which suit and tie to wear tonight. Angela"—he hugged her—"so good to see you. Please tell David I said hello."

"Will do."

He walked away and went upstairs.

Angela turned to Amina. "Girl, so damn fine." She high-fived her. "Have fun tonight, own the room, and try not to be worried about what everyone else thinks. Just enjoy the night with him."

"Got it." Amina gave a thumbs-up.

She walked her friend to the door and wrapped her arms

around her. "Love you, Angie, and thanks again for coming over. It's sort of a zucchini-cucumber hybrid."

Angela's eyes widened. "Damn! I knew it!"

"Got to go, Angie, bye!"

THEY HELD HANDS and walked to the greeting table to find their table number.

"Nate!" Shawn yelled from across the way.

"Oh, there's Shawn. I hope we're not at his table. I can't bear to watch him sit with a date whose name he won't remember on Monday."

She hoped they weren't at his table either. Despite him being the reason this wonderful man was holding her hand, she still couldn't stand him. She'd seen him in action at the gala the last few years, and how he treated women was repulsive. He hooked up with one of her coworkers, and she was devastated when he didn't call her afterward. It was mind-boggling that he and Nate were as close as they were. She just didn't understand how they could be such good friends.

"Hey, guys, thanks so much for coming. I appreciate you being here." Shawn sounded out of breath.

"No problem, man, glad we could make it. Do you know where we're sitting?"

"No idea, but have fun tonight. Swing by and say hi to my mom before you leave."

"Will do."

They started to walk to their table, when Amina noticed some of those stares followed them along the way. She was going to do all she could to ignore them. They both looked incredible, and this was their first night as couple. The last thing she wanted was to be consumed with other people's feelings. She took a deep breath, and held on to Nate's hand a little tighter. He helped Amina to her seat, and he sat down.

"Nate, how did you and Shawn get to be so close? You guys are so different. It doesn't seem like you have a whole lot in common."

A hostess came by with two glasses of red wine.

"I know it seems strange; he's a bit younger than me, very outspoken, a bit rude, but I like Shawn. I mentored him when he matched with our hospital. He hadn't decided on a program yet, and he did some rotations with me. He said I was one of the few doctors that would allow him to do things. It's not easy for African-American doctors in specialty hospitals because there are so few. We lose a lot of them for that reason. They tend to go to larger hospitals because they have a larger level of support. He's incredibly smart, loves medicine, and, knowing that, I wanted to make sure that I could be an ally for him and give him all of the support he needed. Despite him being a jerk on everything else, he's good at this stuff.

"So when it comes to him being honored, I'm here for

him. He's also hilarious. Being in surgery for hours at times can be debilitating. Having him in there with me is a gift. He's the only person who makes me laugh besides you. I try to talk to him about how he treats women, but it's just how he is. I'm sure when the right one comes along, things will change. Shawn, he's an excellent friend. He was there for me with the Stacy drama and all the other stuff that came after. I trust him. I know he's a lot, but at his core, he's a good guy. You got to trust me on that." Nate spoke about Shawn like a big brother would talk about a little brother. He was proud of him. Suddenly, they were joined by two guests at the table.

Nate had a look on his face that Amina had never seen before.

He mumbled under his breath, "I'm going to kill him." He sighed. "Amina, this is Stacy and her husband, Corey. Stacy and Corey, this is my girlfriend, Amina." Stacy tried to fix her face, but Amina saw the disappointment when that word *girlfriend* came out of Nate's mouth. She wasn't sure if it was because he was with someone else or because the someone else was Black.

Stacy was the total opposite of Amina in every way possible—very tall, thin, long dark brown hair, and blue eyes. She was beautiful.

"Nice to meet you both," Amina said.

She could tell Nate was blindsided. The anger rolled off of him. She put her hand on his knee under the table to try to calm him.

"It's so nice to meet you," Stacy said. She tried to sound sweet, but she failed.

"I didn't know you guys were going to be here," Nate said.

"Yeah, Shawn invited me when we played ball last week," Corey said. "He said you would be okay with it, and it was no big deal."

Nate shifted in his seat as Amina rubbed his knee.

"Not sure why he would think you would've had an issue with us coming. I mean, you and Stacy haven't been together for years. I wasn't sure where that was coming from." Corey sounded genuinely confused.

The look on Stacy's face said something very different. She couldn't take her eyes off of Nate, even though her husband sat next to her.

Amina jumped in. "Nate mentioned that you guys have two kids?"

Corey's face brightened, and he showed her pictures of their kids and talked about them. Stacy remained quiet and continued to stare at Nate.

"So how long have you two been together?" Stacy finally asked, her voice filled with judgment and suspicion.

Nate took a deep breath and held Amina's hand. "We've been seeing each other for...what?" He looked at her for a bit of assistance. "Three or four weeks now?" He grinned in the way Amina loved.

"Yeah, that sounds about right." She smiled.

He winked at her. Stacy frowned.

Corey laughed. "Well, you two look great together and very happy."

"Thanks. Hey, Nate, can you come with me for a quick second over to the bar?"

"Sure, babe." He pulled out Amina's chair, and they both left the table.

Once they reached the bar, she asked, "Are you okay? Because you look like you are going to explode right now."

"I'm going to kill him. Why would he not tell me that he invited them? And why would Shawn sit them at the table with us?"

She put her hand on Nate's face and rubbed his beard.

Amina took a breath and tried to wrap her head around all that was happening. She was already doing all she could to overcome the overwhelming glares that followed them around the room, and now this.

"You said she broke up with you. She seems so angry with you."

Nate stepped back and looked in Amina's eyes. "She did! She was the one who cheated on me. She's acting like I did something wrong. The only thing I did wrong was not talking to her about rushing into marriage. But that was it. I never did her wrong when we were together. You don't believe me or something?"

"She just seems really pissed for someone who cheated.

Really odd." Amina turned to look back at the table.

How easy would things be for him if he were still with Stacy?

"I'm not lying to you about what happened."

Amina sighed. So much for a fun night out. "I'm gonna go to the restroom. Did you want me to meet you somewhere?" She needed to be away from him for a moment to clear her head.

"I'll be here at the bar."

Chapter Thirteen

AMINA FIXED HER hair and made sure the makeup job from Angela was still on point. She tried to free her thoughts from the idea that Nate lied to her, but it was hard. She was startled when Stacy walked out of a stall. They made eye contact via the mirror, and Amina wanted to be kind.

"Are you and Corey having a good time tonight?"

Stacy, still with a frown, said, "I guess. How about you and Nate?"

"Umm, we're having an okay time."

"Well, I'm sure things will turn around. I didn't mean to stare, I've just never really seen Nate out with another woman before. Kinda weird." She chuckled.

"Yeah, he told me you guys were together for a long time." Amina gripped the sink.

"We were. Also, he never struck me as the type who would, you know, date outside his race."

"Oh really, why is that?"

"I mean he's not racist or anything—oh, and neither am I. But with him being so obsessed with medicine and all, I figured he would try to be with someone who would make things easier."

Amina felt the heat around her ears as she listened to this woman's microaggressions.

"Let me get back out there. I'm sure Corey is looking for me. Hope you guys have a good night." Stacy left Amina alone in the restroom.

She didn't know what to do. Nate was amazing, sweet and kind, and fulfilled every sexual fantasy she could've ever imagined. And he told the truth about Stacy, but Amina didn't want to be a hinderance to him because of who she was. He loved being a doctor, and she didn't want to do anything to put his career in jeopardy.

Amina found Nate at the bar where she left him. He ordered two old-fashioneds for them as Amina walked up behind him and slid her hand into his.

"Hey," she whispered in his ear, "can we sit down and talk away from the table a bit?"

"Sure, what happened?"

She pointed to a little couch off the bar area with just enough room for them to sit so she could fill him in on what happened with Stacy.

"I told you I wasn't lying," he said as he sipped his drink.

"I know. I'm sorry I doubted you on that. Nate, can I ask you a question?"

"Sure, babe, anything."

Amina sipped her drink and sighed. "Nate, how do you

think people in the hospital would feel about us being together? Like, I'm sure you have events and retreats and things. Do you think they will frown on you for being with me?"

"Are you serious?" he asked.

"Well, yeah."

"Amina, the chief of the hospital is an Asian woman married to Black man. I don't think she would care. Even if she did, why does it matter? I mean, yes, I am the only white man here with a black woman on his arm. I know you feel like a spotlight is on you tonight. I understand." He sighed and adjusted himself on the sofa beside her. "My point is this, babe, I'm not afraid of the spotlight. I'm not afraid to be in a relationship with you. You have to figure out a way to be okay with this. To answer your question, no one would care. It seems the only one who is so stressed over this is you." Nate got up from the sofa and walked away, leaving Amina alone.

Amina sat and stared out the window; it was dark but she could still see the waves from the lake. She closed her eyes and heard his words in her head. She remembered their nights together and how much she enjoyed being with him. Amina couldn't walk away, she couldn't. She had to see where this could go.

Amina sat down next to him at the table and smiled nervously at him. She placed her hand on his knee and kissed his cheek. Yeah, she had to see where this went.

Finally, things got underway to honor Shawn. How extraordinary the event was. It was very cool to see this room filled with Black people there to honor him, especially with him being so young. There weren't enough Black doctors, and for him to be a face that so many kids saw headed into surgery or an appointment was pretty cool. She had to give it up for Shawn. He got up there and accepted his award, something about trailblazing in the world of medicine. He looked very humbled, which was quite a rare thing with him. He was so gracious. He thanked the board that voted for him, and then Amina heard, "Dr. Nathan Moore."

"I'm sure many of you have been wondering who the very tall, white guy is who walked in tonight." Shawn laughed, and the room laughed along with him. "Well, Dr. Moore is my mentor and one of my best friends."

Nate beamed.

Shawn continued, "So when I started working at the children's hospital, which doesn't have a lot of African-American doctors, Dr. Moore became my mentor. He allowed me to scrub in on surgeries, the more simple ones to gain experience. He let me handle his post-ops and take the lead on many of his patients. All of these things are not out of the ordinary. Where Dr. Moore really showed me what type of man he is was when he had a patient and he wanted me to take the lead on the consult, the surgery, the post-op, everything. The father of the patient would not talk to me. He kept talking to Dr. Moore. Dr. Moore kept trying to direct the father to me, and he just wouldn't. Finally, he said to me, 'Shawn, I'm pulling myself of this case.'

"I knew what was happening, but I didn't want to rock the boat. I was a bit nervous about speaking up and complaining. I didn't know how that would've made me look. You know how the whole black tax thing works."

Many in the room nodded, including Amina. She knew all too well.

"Dr. Moore told me, 'You are one of the few in this hospital, and you need to start showing them you belong here. You are a doctor and a brilliant one, and you need to demand respect. Don't be afraid to speak up and be clear. I see what's happening. I don't want you to think that I don't. You have my support. I got your back.'

"I was stunned. Stunned that he would, number one, acknowledge his privilege, and number two, empower me to thrive. That was the day that I knew Dr. Moore was a real one." Shawn looked at Nate.

They smiled and nodded to each other. Nate squeezed Amina's hand as she beamed from ear to ear.

"Dr. Moore continued to give me cases to take the lead on. He wanted me to grow. He helped me find my first place, and he filmed my first solo surgery for my mom. Even though he told me it was for me to use for a review so it wouldn't make me nervous. And when I wanted to figure out a plan to get more young Black kids involved and to learn more about medicine, Dr. Moore was the one who sat down with me to come up with a game plan. Now there are programs in several CPS schools as a result. I say all this to say, Nathan, I appreciate everything you've done for my mom and me. There's no way I could get this honor without all of your care and support. Thanks, bro."

The entire room gave Nate a standing ovation, and he could do nothing but smile, wave, and take it all in. Amina's eyes were filled with tears, and she had to fight them. She didn't want to ruin Angela's makeup job. She was so wrong to think she couldn't do this with him. If there was anyone she could overcome her fears with, it was him.

He turned toward the table and whispered to Amina, "I didn't see that coming, at all."

Shawn continued speaking eloquently about his family, his mom, and his career. He indeed was a brilliant doctor. The reason why their friendship was the way it was started to become much more apparent.

"That was incredible, Nate." She kissed him on the cheek.

"I'm shocked. I'm thrilled and proud of him."

Amina stared at him, so proud to have him in her life. When she pulled her eyes away from him, she looked across the table. Stacy quickly turned her head, but Amina caught her staring at them.

He stood and took Amina's hand once Shawn finished his speech. "We're going to say thank you and congrats to Shawn, and we're out of here, okay?" He looked for approval.

She was ready, and they couldn't get back to the loft fast enough. They walked through the crowd and found Shawn. She couldn't have been happier to be holding Nate's hand.

"Thanks so much for inviting us." She hugged Shawn, something she never thought she would be doing.

"Thanks, bro, that was amazing. I'm very proud of you!"

"All facts, bro, all facts!"

Nate saw Ms. Atkins, Shawn's mom, and walked to her. "I couldn't leave without saying goodbye to the prettiest woman in the room." He smiled at her.

"Oh, Nathan, it's so good to see you. Where have you been? You have to come over for dinner." She wrapped her arms around him like he was her child.

"I know it's been a while. I'll have to take some time to come hang out with you. This is my girlfriend, Amina."

Ms. Atkins smiled. "Hey there, it's so nice to meet you." She hugged Amina too.

"Hello, it's nice to meet you, and congrats. You must be so proud."

"Thank you. I am very proud."

She turned her attention back to Nate, and Shawn joined them. Amina was fascinated with how much everyone loved Nate. Everyone he had a relationship with fell in love with him and wanted to be around him. He seemed magical.

Nate reached for her hand, they posed for a picture, and they headed back to the loft.

She stared at him from the passenger seat. "That really happened with the patient's father?" she asked.

Nate sighed. "Yeah. I stood in the hall so that I could listen when Shawn went back to the room by himself. When he told him, 'I am your doctor, and she is in the best hands possible. You can accept the care that I am going to provide, or you can go elsewhere,' I was so proud of him because the dad was a first-class ass. But Shawn had to know he wouldn't be the last like that, you know, sadly. He had to start learning how to deal with it, but he didn't want to appear problematic or be judged by the higher-ups if he spoke up. Needless to say, his confidence is 100 percent all good. Proud of him."

"So you're truly like a super doctor," Amina imitated, posing like a superhero.

He laughed. "Not at all, but I understood the dynamics of him being a Black man in that space at that moment. I needed to stand up for him by getting out of the way. He needed to take the lead, and I needed to follow. The best thing for me to do was to let him know I saw what was happening and I had his back."

"That is quite possibly the sexiest thing you have ever said!"

He winked at her.

Once they got back to the loft, he didn't say a word. Amina didn't know what to do or what to say. All she knew was that she wanted him. He looked down at her and gently grabbed her chin and grinned. She looked in his gorgeous eyes and smiled at him; he was such a beautiful person. She couldn't believe her luck. He reached for her hand and led her upstairs where, with his mouth on her neck, he began to very slowly unzip her dress. Amina tried to keep her calm, but she felt ready to explode.

He whispered in her ear, "Even though you looked so beautiful and sexy in this dress tonight, I have wanted to take it off you since you came down the stairs." He kissed her ear and then her neck, and Amina could no longer keep her calm.

She turned around and stepped out of her dress to face him. She undid his bow tie, and he took off his jacket on his own. She slowly unbuttoned his shirt and inhaled the smell of him. She looked up at him, and he smiled down at her.

They kissed each other gently and enjoyed each moment. She pushed Nate down on the bed and climbed on top of him, and removed his undershirt. She placed her lips on every inch of his skin she saw. Nate sat up and flipped her over. He moved to her breasts, where he delighted in touching them, and placed her hard nipples in his mouth. Amina's control was gone. He moved into her, and her breath caught. He softly whispered her name into her ear, and she smiled at how good he made her feel. She was not sure how long he made love to her, but she didn't want it to stop. It could've gone on and on for hours and hours, and even then, she wasn't sure if she could get enough of him.

Chapter Fourteen

AMINA SAT ON the kitchen island, wearing his shirt from the night before. She tried to keep her poise while he stood in the kitchen wearing only sweatpants. She had to figure out how to stay calm and look at his perfect body without wanting to jump on him all the time. Her body was overheated around him, and her head was constantly replaying their moments in the bedroom. She wanted more of it all the time.

"So, what's your plan for today?" Nate faced her with coffee in hand.

"Um, nothing major. Going to go home, start some laundry, clean my house, and see my dad for a couple of hours. Nothing too big. You?"

"Sunday lunch—or is it an early dinner?—with my parents. I have to drive up to Evanston to their place. After I take you home, going to hit the gym and then head out there to see them." He leaned over the island, and Amina uncrossed her legs.

"Oh, would it be easier for me to get an Uber? I'm sort

of out of your way."

He slid close and stood in between her legs. "No chance. I won't be seeing you again until Wednesday so I'm going to hang on to these last little moments a bit." He put his hand on her face and kissed her in his favorite way. "So, are we good on all the race stuff?" He kissed her again.

Amina traced her fingers across his chest and grinned. "Yeah, I'm going to do my best with all of this."

She wrapped her legs around him, and he picked her up and carried her over to the couch. He unbuttoned the two buttons on the shirt and made love to her. They held nothing back that morning. It was an excellent way to start the day.

Amina held Nate's hand as he drove her home. She stared at his exquisite profile, but he was very quiet. She stroked her thumb across his strong hand, and he kissed hers but never said a word.

"Are you okay?" she asked.

"Yeah, just gonna miss you, that's all."

When he pulled in the driveway, they sat quietly savoring the last little moments of their weekend.

"Have there been any more leads on Omar?" he asked as he stared at her house.

"Just a couple of tips on him still being in the area."

"When did they tell you that?"

"Yesterday. I'm sorry I didn't tell you. The day got away from me, and it just slipped my mind."

"Amina, you can't let stuff like that slip your mind. What if he's in your house right now?"

"I'm sure everything is fine. The police have someone patrolling the area, and it's almost better if he shows up because then they can catch him."

"Well, why don't you call him so he can show up at your door?"

Amina got out of the car, took her bags from the back seat, and slammed the car door without a word.

"Amina, I'm sorry. I just don't want anything to happen to you." Nate hopped out of the car and followed her to the door.

"I'm already stressed about this and us. I was caught up with everything yesterday and forgot. I'm sorry. I don't need you being an asshole about all of this."

He grabbed her and turned her around to face him. "Listen, I'm sorry I said that. I'm just worried, the longer he's out there. It all just makes me nervous. I know you don't need me making things worse by asking a whole bunch of questions about it. Just please, keep me posted, okay? I care about you." He stroked her face. "I would be devastated if something happened to you." He sighed. "I'm sorry I snapped at you. I shouldn't have reacted that way. I know it's not what you need."

"The snide remarks about this can't happen again," she said.

"Done."

She hugged and kissed him. She knew he meant it.

"Forgiven, and thank you. I promise I will do a better job at keeping you updated."

He grabbed her bags while she unlocked her door. He walked all through her house. He checked every room, every closet, under the bed, behind the couch, and everywhere a person could hide. He also asked Amina if he could see the cameras and how they worked. He wanted to know what to look for and how to review everything.

"Thanks for checking everything. I have meetings all day for the next couple of days. I'm going to miss you, Nate." She stood with her arms wrapped around his massive body.

"I'm gonna miss you too, babe." He put his chin on top of her head. "I have to get out of here. My mom can be annoying if I show up late. I'll call you later. Enjoy the day with your dad. Can you tell him I said hi?"

"Will do." She walked him to the door.

He leaned down, lifted her chin, and gave her a long kiss goodbye.

HE ARRIVED AT his parents' late, but they'd still be happy to see their only child. He always thought it was funny that his parents had this huge house and it was only the three of them.

"Hello! The best son in the world is home!" He laughed as he walked in the door.

His mom jogged into the foyer and hugged him. "Nathan!" she yelled and held him tight. "Oh, it's so good to see you."

"Did you see me at all, Mom?"

"Oh, stop it! So happy you made it home to have dinner with us."

"Mom, why are you acting like I just returned home from war? I just saw you a couple of weeks ago."

"Well, for a mom, a couple of weeks is a couple of years. I always miss this handsome face. Even though you keep covering it up with this beard." She shook his chin.

He laughed. "Where's Dad?"

"In the kitchen, working on dinner." She put her arm through his and they walked to the kitchen.

"Hey, Dad," Nate said and hugged him.

"Hey, son, how are you doing?"

"Doing pretty good." Nate grinned.

"How long are you staying with us tonight?"

"Probably going to head back out after dinner. My first surgery is at nine a.m. But I want to get home to go over some patient files." This was total BS; he wasn't in the mood to be interrogated about when they could expect grandchildren.

"Well, I was hoping you could watch some football with me." He patted him on the back.

"Nathan, I was reading through the Sunday paper this morning, and look at what I saw on the front page of the

Lifestyles section." She held up a picture of him, Amina, and Shawn holding his award, with his date and his mom.

Nate, for a moment, tried to remember when the picture was taken, but all he focused on was how beautiful Amina looked. Even on newspaper print, she looked stunning. He felt so complete being with her. He missed her; the next few days were going to be awful away from her.

"Can I see that?" he asked his mom.

"Sure."

The caption was something about the African-American Association of Doctors, with Honoree Dr. Shawn Atkins, his date, Dr. Nathan Moore, his girlfriend Amina Wright, and he stopped reading. He didn't need to read anything more. He wanted to make sure that whatever was written was correct, and it was, but he knew this dinner with his parents was about to be a nightmare.

"So, who is Amina Wright? And why are we finding out about her from a picture in the newspaper?" His mom raised her eyebrows and poked at her food on the plate.

"Mom. I didn't expect this to be in the newspaper, first of all. Second, I didn't want to say anything until I knew for sure she is someone I want to be in my life. What would be the point of talking to you about her, and then we ended up not seeing each other anymore?" He tried to be logical.

"Nathan, you know I don't care about any of that. I care that you felt you couldn't share that you were seeing someone with me."

"Would you leave that boy alone?" his dad said. "Son, she's beautiful." He gave Nate an approving smile that only a dad could provide.

"What does she do?" his mom asked.

"She works for the Bulls in community and urban development. When you see the players visiting patients at the hospitals or handing out food and school supplies, she's the one who sets up those events. She's responsible for which players are there. That's what she does."

"All of that sounds fine and good. The most important question is, does she like basketball?" his dad asked.

"Oh, she loves it, Dad. She would talk about it for hours if she could. It's something we talk about a lot." He loved talking about Amina. How happy she made him and how good he felt being around her.

"How is it with the race thing? I mean, have you guys had any issues? We raised you to see color and be respectful of everyone, but not everybody was raised that way," Mom said.

"So far, the only thing we've dealt with is some stares here and there. Which Amina is having a hard time with. I'm the first white man she's dated, so the only issue has been her adjusting to that. She's worried about my job, and if me being with her will be an issue. I told her it wouldn't."

"Well, it's an adjustment. It's different. It's an unavoidable thing—it can't be denied."

"I know, I've told her to be honest about how she feels,

and she's doing that. So we're just taking it all one day at time. But, I really like her."

"Well, as your dad said, she's quite beautiful. Are you planning on bringing her for Thanksgiving lunch?"

Why would I subject her to being tortured?

"Not sure yet, Mom. We haven't talked about any of that stuff yet."

His dad got up from the table. "Well, let's go see if any more of the games are on so we can watch a bit before you leave."

Nate almost ran from the dining room.

Chapter Fifteen

NATE MET UP with Shawn after a long, busy day at the hospital, and he had a lengthy workout. When he got to his car, he looked at his phone. He had three text messages and four missed calls from her. He didn't bother to read them; he just called her right back.

"Nate!" She sounded scared and out of breath.

"Baby, what's wrong? What happened?"

"He was here! Last night, he was here outside of the house. The cameras caught him. He walked outside of the house while I was upstairs. And before you ask, yes, I called the police. They are patrolling the neighborhood. I called Tina, my dad's nurse, and told her to keep an eye out and do not let anyone in the house. I called Amir and told him, too, but who knows what he'll do with the information."

Nate squeezed his hands around his steering wheel. He hated to hear her hurting. He would give anything to take all of this from her.

"Please come to the loft," Nate pleaded with her.

He didn't want her at her house at all, let alone by herself.

"Okay. I was going to ask—"

"You never have to," he interrupted. "I'm sorry I didn't answer. I was at the gym with Shawn and didn't have my phone on me."

"It's okay." Amina sniffled.

"No, it's not okay. You needed me, and I wasn't there."

"But you're here now."

"How soon will you be at the loft?" he asked.

"Um, well, I have to pack."

"Amina, pack for the week, or longer. You can stay as long as you want." He wanted to do whatever he could to make sure she was safe. If that meant she would stay with him temporarily, so be it.

"Okay, it will be at least an hour or so until I get there."

He overheard the police talking to her, and they were glad to hear that she was leaving home. He started to relax a bit.

"They have to catch this asshole."

"I know. It seems the police are doing everything they can, and the neighborhood is helping too. Right now, they just want me somewhere safe. I'll get to you as soon as I can." She sounded so small, so wounded.

He hurried to get to the loft to make sure he was there for her.

When Nate got to the loft, he cleaned up a bit, checked the fridge, and made sure it was fully loaded. She called from the lobby, and the security guard walked her up. She looked so shaken up. He hated to see her like this. He took her bags from the security guard. As soon as he closed the door, he wrapped her in his arms as she broke down.

She eventually let Nate go and he took everything upstairs while she took a long, hot shower and tried to calm down and relax. She sat on the couch, curled up next to him while they watched whatever was on ESPN. She didn't have a whole lot to say. When the doorbell buzzed for the food, she jumped.

"It's all right, babe. It's all right."

He answered the door, paid for the food, but Amina moved away from the door.

She walked over to the dining room, sat down. Nate quietly got all of the dishes for them, a bottle of wine, and sat down next to her. Tonight he wanted to be close to her.

"I was so scared looking at that security footage, Nate." She took a few bites of food and a deep breath. "I went into my office to make sure I had everything I needed for my meetings tomorrow, like Post-its." She sighed. "I took a look at the footage because I haven't checked it in a day or so. Then I saw him." She took a few more bites of food and deep breaths. "He was walking along the side of the house. Then he was on the porch like he was trying to figure out how to get in. Then I had to call you and tell you everything." She turned to him. "I keep thinking I'm not good enough for you because of everything that's happening with this mess I'm in, and sooner or later, you're going to figure that out. I feel like at any moment you're going to tell me that's it. You're done, and we'll be over. You didn't sign up for this. You didn't sign up for my problems, and all my fears around you being white. It's all just such a mess. Everything would be so much easier for you if you just walked away."

"Oh, babe. I made a decision a while ago that I am all in, and we will figure our way through it all. I'm not going anywhere. You are the best thing for me, more than you could ever imagine."

She didn't say much else during dinner. She finished her food and stepped upstairs and called her boss.

"How did everything go?" His voice was soft, almost a whisper.

"He said that I could do everything online and I don't have to come in, so all of this"—she twirled her finger around the loft—"will be my office for the week." Amina sounded so relieved.

"That's great. I would've been so worried about you. I'm glad that all worked out." He kissed her forehead and turned the TV off. "You must be beat."

"I am. I'm exhausted."

"Come on." They stood up, he locked up the loft, and they walked upstairs.

They climbed in the bed, and he turned on the game on the TV in the bedroom. He lay down, and Amina lay down next to him. She placed her head on his chest, his arms around her, and she stayed there until she drifted off to sleep.

Chapter Sixteen

NATE WAS THRILLED. The surgery with Ryan, Shawn, and an oncologist was done, and it went well. They got the whole tumor in her arm, she was going to keep it, and her scans were just about clear. Mr. and Mrs. Harris hugged him in the waiting room. He was going to miss them. He'd gotten so close to Ryan and the rest of her family, but he was happy that she would be going home soon.

He was mostly done for the day. He grabbed files of some new patients who were going to be coming his way. Made sure he had everything he needed since he was on call tomorrow, and he was on his way home. When he arrived at the loft, Amina was in the bedroom, getting ready for dinner.

"Hey, beautiful." He smiled at her when he made it upstairs and kissed her. "No hoodie and yoga pants?" he asked.

"No, I figured I'd save that look for tomorrow when you're with me the whole day." She grinned at him.

"I will look forward to that." He was so happy to see her spirits were up after everything that happened yesterday.

He could tell that she was still a little on edge, but she had started to look more like herself. They ventured out of the loft to grab a bite to eat, something simple. They walked over to a bar not too far away. She held Nate's hand a little tighter, and she looked around at every person who walked by. She usually paid attention to the stares, but this time it felt different. This situation with Omar had taken a little bit of joy from them. Amina still laughed and smiled, but there was a level of caution she didn't have before.

But he didn't want to impose and keep asking how she felt about everything, so he let it go. He chose a table far away from the door so that she wouldn't be distracted or afraid of every person who walked through. They held hands and gazed at each other while he filled her in on all of the details about Ryan's surgery. Once they were done, he paid the bill. They went straight back to the loft.

Nate took off her coat, then kissed her on the neck like he always did. He hung up their coats and joined her on the couch.

"Amina"—he reached out and held her hand—"are you okay?" He knew how loaded that question was.

She turned to him, kissed him on the lips. She placed her hand on his face and studied him while she stroked his beard. "I'm trying to be. I'm trying to be normal and feel normal, but it's just this thing that's sitting in the back of my mind. It's hard to shake, you know?"

He put his hand on her face as he listened. He knew

what he wanted to say at that moment, but he was afraid.

"I want to thank you, though."

"Thank me for what?" he asked.

"For being here for me. For not forcing me to talk, for listening to me, allowing me to stay here. For not running away from me with everything that's going on. For being all in."

"I'm happy I can be here for you. Everything will be okay, babe." He stroked her cheek with his thumb.

She gently moved her thumb across his lips. Everything around them slowed down, and nothing else mattered. Not Omar, their jobs, nothing. Just them. He smiled against her lips, and she put her hands into the scruff of his beard, then leaned forward and kissed him. He pulled away from her, looked into her eyes, took her hand, and walked upstairs to his bedroom.

They took their time as they undressed each other and took each other in with long glances, smiles, and joy. Nate gently placed Amina on the bed, and kissed her from the tip of her toes, along her legs, to her thighs, her breasts, until finally he reached her lips. He pushed himself inside as Amina moaned in delight.

EARLY THE NEXT morning, Amina's eyes flickered open as she heard Nate moving around the bedroom. "If the goal was to leave and not wake me up, you're not doing a very good job." She laughed.

"I was trying not to wake you. I got a call from the hospital, emergency surgery. I'm going to be there for a while. I'm on call today, and since I'm already there, it's not going to make any sense to come home."

"I understand. I'll miss you."

"I'll miss you too. Have a good meeting, and I'll try to get back home as soon as I can." He looked under the covers at her naked body and grinned.

"Don't look at me like that." She giggled.

Nate kissed her forehead and left for the hospital.

By nine a.m., Nate had already been in surgery on a girl who fell off of her bunkbed. Another kid stabbed himself with some scissors, and another needed an ACL repair. He lay down in his office and tried to get a bit of rest until the next text came through that told him where he needed to be in the hospital. He was about to close his eyes when there was a knock at the door. He sighed, frustrated.

"Come on in." He sat up and thought it was a nurse or a resident dropping off a file on a patient, or Shawn, but he rarely knocked.

Nate was shocked to see who had walked into his office. It was Omar. Nate was trying to figure out what to do when Omar finally spoke.

"Probably not the smartest thing for a picture to turn up in a newspaper." Omar sneered at Nate as he dropped the newspaper on his table with the photo of Nate and Amina faceup. "I keep trying to get to her, and you guys took that stupid picture, Dr. Moore." He spat out his name.

Omar was tall, although not as tall as Nate. He could see how Amina would've been attracted to him years ago. But now he looked unkept and unhinged. Nate was unprepared and frightened by what this man could do to him.

"What the hell do you want?" Nate finally got out of his mouth.

"I want her," Omar said.

"Amina doesn't want you. Why can't you just leave her the hell alone?" Nate stood from his couch.

"She left me and made me feel like I was nothing, and I want to show her how wrong she was. I want her to feel the pain I felt when she left me."

"There was nothing wrong about her leaving you. You were the one who decided to put your hands on her. You want to prove her wrong? How, exactly? By stalking her and breaking into her house? What exactly is the plan here? What is coming to my job and talking to me going to do?" Nate hoped that of all days, Shawn would barge in.

"I want you to help me get to her." Omar was calm as he walked around Nate's office.

He picked up a picture of Nate's parents.

"I'm not helping you do shit! You need to get the hell out of my office and this hospital," Nate shouted.

Omar just smiled and tossed the framed picture down. "Oh, I think you will. I can keep coming here and start harming your staff, or better yet, your patients. Or, I know, I can move on to start harming Angela and David. I know how much Amina loves them both."

Nate lunged at Omar and slammed him up against the wall. He reeked from hiding out and sleeping who knew where. "You will not lay a finger on her or anyone else! Do you hear me, you piece of shit?! Leave her alone! She doesn't want to have anything to do with you!" he screamed in Omar's face.

He didn't care if people outside of his office heard what was going on. He wanted this guy out of all of their lives.

"It's not about what she wants. It's about what I want, and I want her."

Nate still had Omar pinned against the wall when Shawn came into his office.

"What's going on? Nate, you good?"

"No! Get the police!" He had never been more grateful for spending hours in the gym.

His strength and rage were enough to keep Omar hemmed up against the wall until security came.

"Nate! What the hell is going on?" Shawn asked.

"Just get the police, Shawn!" Nate shouted.

Shawn rushed down the hall to get security. Finally, the police arrived and arrested Omar.

Nate tried to catch his breath. "This is the asshole who's been stalking Amina," he said to Shawn. "We haven't talked in a bit, and I have to catch you up on some things, but this is the guy. There's so much more to the story, and I can't get into all of that right now."

Omar smiled when the police removed him from Nate's office. He apparently didn't have any remorse for the continued pain he brought to her.

"Wow, this is crazy as hell! Have you called Amina? What's going to happen now?" Shawn asked.

"I have no idea, bro. He just showed up in my office, and all of this happened. Not sure what to do right now. I'm on call."

Shawn put both of his hands up. "I got it. Find her. Let her know what's going on. I got you."

"I owe you."

"The list is getting long." Shawn smirked at his friend.

Nate filed his report with the police, and he always talked to Shawn about his patients, so he didn't need to update him too much. "Thanks again, Shawn."

"No problem. Find Amina and let her know what's going. I'm glad that guy is getting locked up and won't be causing her any more problems."

When Nate got to his car, his adrenaline finally calmed down. He felt sick, and his head started to hurt at the sheer thought of that man anywhere near Amina. He called her.

"Hey, Nate—"

"Babe, where are you? Are Angela and David with you? I know you mentioned spending some time with them after your meetings today? If you're out, I need you to get back home as soon as possible. I will explain everything when I get there. Are you okay?" he asked, out of breath.

"We didn't leave yet. We'll stay here until you get here, and we're fine. Are you okay? Did something happen to you? You're scaring me."

"Good. Glad you guys are okay. I'll explain everything when I get there. Be there soon, and I'm fine."

He hung up with a bit of relief. Omar was in police custody, and Amina was at home with people she loved. He pulled out of the parking garage.

Chapter Seventeen

"MINA, WHAT'S WRONG? What happened?" Angela asked.

"I don't know. That was Nate, and I have never heard him sound like that before. He said not to leave, and he would explain everything when he got here." She tried to remain calm, but she was scared.

"Is there somewhere David can go? In case whatever it is he needs to tell us is something he doesn't need to know or hear?"

"Yeah, he can go upstairs to the bedroom, and don't worry. It's clean."

"Thank goodness. I mean, I can tell by looking at you it's been going down on the regular." Angela snickered and poured a drink.

"Yes, and it's so damn good!" Amina laughed. "Don't worry. All the whips, chains, feathers, and leather have been put away."

"I wouldn't be mad at you if I walked up there and saw it. I'd be like get it, Mina." They high-fived each other.

Amina was so grateful for David's Switch and his eagerness to put his headphones on when he saw them together.

"Ah, yes, Nate is amazing. Incredibly amazing. Things have been going quite well. I'm glad too. I didn't think I would ever be able to truly see past all the race stuff, but it's getting a little easier because he's been so great. He's never ordered me around like that before." She shook her head free of scary thoughts and tried to move on.

Nate walked through the door. He looked pale and stressed. Whatever he needed to tell her, it wasn't good.

"Hey, Dr. Nathan." David removed his headphones.

"Hey, dude." Nate gave him a fist bump. "How are you doing?"

He took time and caught up with David, which Amina appreciated. She loved seeing them together. David missed having a man who had similar interests as him in his life. Amir would hang out with David from time to time, but they never really connected.

"What do you think it is?" Angela whispered to Amina while they watched them from the kitchen.

"I have no idea. He looks a little shaken up for sure."

"I'd love to hang out with you for a bit, David, but I have to talk to your aunt Mina and your mom about something important, okay?"

"I know. I overheard you have to talk to my mom and Auntie Mina about something. I put my headphones on, so I'm not sure what else they said after that."

"Hey, you." He hugged and kissed Amina. "Hey, Angela. It's good to see you. How are you?"

"I'm good, Nate. So, what's going on?"

He pointed upstairs. When they got to the bedroom, Amina pointed to the bed for her and Angela to have a seat. Angela took her friend's hand while they sat on bed waiting for Nate to explain what the heck was going on.

She watched him as he paced around the bedroom searching for the right words to explain all that just happened.

"Nate, we can't read your mind, you're going to have to use actual words and let us know what's going on," Angela said.

"I was sitting in my office, just finished like three surgeries, about to shut my eyes before I got called into another one and guess who walked into my office?"

Amina put her hands up and shook her head, clueless.

"Omar," he blurted out.

Amina froze.

"Omar walked into my office today."

"Oh my God, are you serious?" Angela grabbed Amina's hand.

"Yes. I was stunned when he walked in. I had no idea what to do. I'm not sure how he made his way through the hospital. My guess is he lied about who he was, considering the police are looking for him."

"What did he want?" Amina's voice quivered, and her

blood ran cold.

"Well, the picture in the newspaper was how he found me. You can Google my name and find out what hospital I work at. He said he just wanted you. He wanted you to see he's not some loser you just left but the man he is now. He wants you to know you made a mistake, and he's going to make you pay for the mistake you made. He started making threats about how he was going to start harming my staff, then harming Angela and David. After that, I slammed his ass against the wall. Shawn came in, got security and the police, and they arrested him." His voice started to sound like his own again.

"That's good, right?" Angela asked. "I mean, he's off the streets, and they can keep him, right? Because he violated the restraining order when he came to your house."

Amina sat silent. She was numb. "I can't believe he went to your job. If he was willing to go to your job, he's willing to harm everyone I love. I feel like I'm putting everyone I'm close to in danger. I'm afraid that something awful is going to happen to everyone because of me."

Nate got down on his knees in front of her, and Angela put her head on her shoulder.

"I'm not sure how his arrest works. I'll have to call Detective Ross if he hasn't called me already and see what he says. I mean, I hope Omar's locked up long-term, but there's no guarantee. It's probably best if everyone just stayed away from me so they don't get hurt. It's the only way everyone can be safe." She felt like a failure.

Omar was still destroying her life. This was absolutely the last thing Nate needed. The Black girlfriend bringing fights and exes to the hospital.

"You're talking crazy right now, Mina," Angela said. "You know I'm not going anywhere, and neither is Nate."

But Nate didn't say a word.

She went downstairs, and she had two messages from the detective who worked on her case. She called him back, and he needed her to come with Nathan to the police station closest to the hospital as soon as possible. Amina went upstairs and told them what was going on, but Nate had a hard time meeting her eyes.

The car ride to the police station was quiet. What if she was required to come face-to-face with Omar?

The lead detective met with them at the police station and explained that Omar tried to press assault charges against Nathan, but his court-appointed lawyer advised it was a bad idea. That would open up a whole can of worms he surely didn't want to be opened. Nathan couldn't press any trespassing charges because Omar came into a public place. Nathan also didn't have a restraining order against him, so he couldn't press charges on that either. However, Amina could press charges because he was caught after he broke into her home. He could be held on those charges.

"For how long?" Nate asked.

"Well, definitely through the holiday," Detective Ross

said.

"And after that?" Amina asked.

"We'll have to wait and see. All of these charges can vary from six months to six years, depending on a variety of factors. But, for right now, you have a bit of relief. Hopefully, we can extend it to you. He's off the streets. If anything changes, I will let you know."

"Thank you so much, sir." Amina shook his hand.

She reached for Nate's hand to walk out of the station, but he did not grab it. He walked straight to the door without looking at her. Amina climbed into Nate's SUV and his anger was palpable. She looked out the window while they drove through the city, with her mind racing about what to say to him. Everything that came to mind didn't seem like it was right.

He grabbed some pizza and thanked Angela for ordering it when they got back to the loft. He escaped into video games with David, and Amina filled Angela in on what happened at the police station. She sat on the bed clinging to her friend as she spoke.

"Angie, what do I do? What do I say to him? How do I get him to understand that what I said to him was about him being safe?"

"I'm not sure, Mina. I know that's what you meant, but I could see in his eyes that's not what he heard."

Amina curled up on the bed, and stared out the window searching for any form of solace while Angela left her alone with her thoughts.

Finally, it was time for David and Angela to leave for the night.

"Thanks so much for coming over, guys. Sorry the day's plans were ruined."

"Thanks, Dr. Nath—I mean Nate, for letting me hang out and play video games."

"No problem, dude. Whenever you want, just let me know."

"Now, don't complain when he comes to this loft all the time looking for you," Angela said.

She walked over to Amina, who sat on the arm of the couch, and gave her a long hug. Nate thanked them again, and they were gone. He turned and stood with his back against the door, his eyes fixated on her.

She sighed. "I know why you're angry with me. I'm sorry. Obviously, I want to be with you."

"Is it obvious? Instead of you thinking of me, or wondering how we can do this *together* if Omar isn't locked up, the first thing you think is, *Well, I'll just leave, and everyone and everything is fine.* After I have repeatedly told you that I was all in no matter what, how is that even possible? I mean, how could you think that? Do you know how hurtful that is to me? Especially considering I could have lost my job today, my career, dealing with your bullshit!" He started upstairs.

Amina followed him. "I'm sorry, Nathan. I was in shock. I didn't know how to respond to the news about Omar. I felt overwhelmed by everything. It was too much. Everything awful that I could've imagined has happened."

"So, your response is to tell me that you're gone. Come on, Amina, that doesn't make any sense."

"So, now I'm stupid for even thinking the best way to protect people I care about and keep them safe from a psycho is to keep them away from me so he won't do anything to harm them?" Every word he spoke punched her in the gut.

Her biggest fear was causing him embarrassment because of who she was, losing him—and it was all happening.

"You can't just give up like that. If we're going to be together, you can't just turn your back on me."

"Nathan, I want you in my life. I want to be with you. I would have been devastated if Omar had harmed you. If there was anything I could do to protect you, to keep you out of harm's way, I would try to do it even if it meant giving you up. It would hurt like hell, but I would do it."

"No. I don't understand that. I don't." He sat on his bed and stared out the window.

Amina rushed down the stairs, grabbed her coat, and stormed out of the loft to clear her head. She stalked through the windy streets of the city. Why couldn't Nate understand what she was saying? The wind whipped around her body as she pulled her coat closed.

On the other hand, Nate was scared for her and for himself.

She stood on a bridge and stared out at the lake. He was willing to put it all on the line for her. She smiled when she thought of being in his arms, how protected she felt.

Omar would not take this away from her.

She turned around and hurried back to his loft. She needed to be with Nate, and they needed to figure out how to move forward together.

She found Nate cleaning up in the loft. Amina hung up her coat and slid onto the island counter. He turned to face her.

"How was the walk?" he asked.

"It was good. Cold."

Nate nodded, and Amina shifted herself on the counter to find the words to say to him. He tossed a towel on the counter and moved to stand in front of her. It was became increasingly difficult for her to think with him so close. She felt the full weight of his eyes upon her.

"Nate, I'm sorry I ran out of here. I—"

"Hang on," he interrupted. "Let me go first."

Amina nodded.

"Amina, I'm sorry. I think all the adrenaline from everything that happened made it hard for me to see this from all angles. And I'm sorry for that. But hearing you say that you would just walk away was tough to hear. I understand why you would say that. I'm sorry for handling things the way I did."

Amina sighed and pulled Nate into her arms. "Babe, I

am so sorry for making you feel that way. For making you think I didn't want to be with you anymore. You were so brave to do what you did for me today. And I'm so grateful to have you in my life to take that kind of risk. I—"

Nate stopped her with a long, soft kiss.

"Amina, please know that I would never want to do or say anything to hurt you."

"I know, Nate, I know."

She leaned her forehead against his, and he slid between her legs. Amina wanted to enjoy as many of these moments as she could with him. She stroked his beard and moved to kiss him.

Nate pulled away from her kiss and sighed.

"What's on your mind?" Amina asked.

"I just need you to promise that when things get hard, because relationships always have some hard spots, you can't be so quick to toss in the towel."

She stared at him, gobsmacked. They were making up, and things were heading in the right direction.

"Nate, if I need to make sure you're okay, I'm going to do what I see is right."

"And that means giving up?"

She moved off the island and out of his embrace. Amina paced around his kitchen searching for the right words.

"I don't see it that way," she mumbled.

"I know, but there has to be a better way of communicating that doesn't involve the knee-jerk reaction of 'let's just end things.' Do you think we can agree to not do that?" Nate moved close to Amina, slid his arms around her, and placed his chin on her shoulder.

"Is this something we need to resolve right at this moment?" She turned around to face him, and smiled when she stared into his eyes, hoping they could move away from this conversation. She just wanted him, and wanted to feel him everywhere she could.

Nate smiled. "I think we can talk more about this later," he whispered against her neck.

They kissed each other, slow but urgent.

She stood, took his hand, and walked him upstairs to the bedroom. They frantically undressed each other like kids unwrapping presents on Christmas morning.

Afterward, he went downstairs to make sure everything was locked up and all the lights were off. Amina was thrilled to take in the full sight of him as he returned to the bedroom. *Damn, there's just muscle everywhere.* Even his ass was perfection. He climbed back in the bed and wrapped his arms around her. She lay with her head nestled in his chest and let out a sigh. She tried to ignore the nagging feeling in the back of her mind. Amina just wanted to soak up her time with him, even if she couldn't commit to what he wanted.

"You know, I didn't know if you were going to come back when you left. I was scared." He intertwined her fingers in his.

"Honestly, the moment I saw you when I walked in, I

knew we had to fix this." She laughed, and so did he. "I know I scared you."

He reached out and kissed her.

"Nate, tonight was my worst fear coming true—Omar going to the hospital to hurt you. You saw the worst parts of my life that would push you away. Plus, you know how sensitive I am about us being together." She paused. "I feel like I have been waiting on the other shoe to drop."

"Which is why you have to talk to me," he whispered.

She leaned her head against his. Quietly, they listened to each other breathe.

AMINA DECIDED TO go out to a bakery while he slept and surprise him with donuts the next morning. He'd looked so tired when she walked back into the loft, and she wanted him to get some rest. She slid out of bed and tiptoed into the shower. Amina stood with her eyes closed, letting the hot water wash over her body. She could still feel his body pressed against hers, his breath against her skin.

"Good morning, babe," he whispered and kissed her shoulder and her neck.

Amina opened her eyes, surprised at his presence.

"Hey, did I wake you? I'm sorry." The heat rose between them as he wrapped his arms around her.

"Best sleep I've had in a few days. I heard you in here and decided to join you."

He smiled against her skin. Amina leaned her head against him and closed her eyes as his hands moved over her body. He massaged her breasts, and she felt him rise behind her.

She turned to face him. "I was trying to surprise you with donuts." She smiled and stroked her hands around his firm flesh.

He kissed her deeply as the water washed over them both. He picked her up, held her against the wall, and made passionate love to her.

An hour later, they walked down to the bakery and were surprised by how busy it was.

"I'll go grab a table by the window. You know what I like." He gave her a quick kiss on the lips and moved quickly to grab the table before anyone could take it.

She saw the many eyes that followed him across the room. *He's all mine, ladies.* Amina grinned to herself.

"So, my mom called me yesterday, and she wanted to know if I was bringing you over for the holiday. It's pretty small, me being the only child and all. When you knock it out the park the first time, why try again, right?"

Amina nearly choked on her coffee, and he laughed.

His hands never stopped moving when he talked. "We eat early, like around two. So we can go there and still visit your family, too, if you want. Would you be okay with that?"

"Are we ready for the whole meeting of the families?" she

asked.

"Yeah, I think we're ready."

"This has a holiday movie written all over it. But that's fine. I'm off this whole week, so if you want to stay at my place or the loft, I'm good with either. I just want us to be together."

"Well, lucky for you, I'm off this week too. I'd like to stay with you. I like your place. It'll be nice being in a neighborhood for a few days instead of being trapped by a bunch of buildings. Just have to pack up some clothes."

He leaned in and kissed her.

"DO YOU THINK we should show up with a dish or something?" Amina asked Nate the morning of Thanksgiving.

She was determined to not let her nerves get the best of her, but she had no idea what to expect. She'd tossed and turned all night, frightened of the day ahead of her.

"I think we can bring a bottle of wine. She'd appreciate that."

Amina nodded as Nate's voice traveled upstairs to her bedroom. She wanted to make sure she made a good first impression. She cared so much for him, and she wanted things work. Still, she was unsure how his parents would handle their only son showing up with a woman who was Black.

NATE PACED THE living room waiting for Amina to emerge from her bedroom. He had enjoyed every single moment with her over the last few days. She cooked for him and tried to show him how to cook lasagna, because he always wanted to learn how to make it. They started binge-watching shows on Netflix and Hulu, and in between made love. He was grateful for every single moment and so happy he hadn't thrown it all away.

"Amina! We really have to go!" He grew impatient as he waited for her to come downstairs.

"I'm coming!" she shouted at him.

"You have been saying that for the last ten minutes!"

This time she meant it. Nate heard her coming down the steps, and it was worth the wait.

He whistled when he saw her. "You look amazing."

She wore a long skirt, heeled boots, a turtleneck, and her locs were half up and half down and curly. She was flawless.

"How am I supposed to leave the house when you come downstairs looking like this?" He grinned.

"Easy, your mom will be pissed if you're late coming home with your Black girlfriend for Thanksgiving." She smiled. "But thanks."

He smiled, kissed her cheek, and they walked out of the house to head to his parents' house.

When they pulled into the driveway, Nate started to feel a little nervous. He'd never brought home the Black woman he dated previously. His father's best friend was a Black man, and his mother had been quite involved with Civil Rights. Still he was a ball of nerves. Not only did he have this hurdle to conquer, he had a few more to jump when he had dinner with her family later in the day.

"Are you okay, Nate?" Amina asked.

"Just a little nervous. How are you feeling?"

"I'm trying really hard not to, but I'm freaking out a little bit." She chuckled. "I mean, they have this amazing, compassionate, feminist, and socially aware son. As long as they're not horrible, raging racists or sexists, I think things will be fine." She laughed. "I'm pretty sure they're not any of those things." She winked at him. "Still, I can't help but to be a little bit on edge with everything. This whole day is a lot."

"Well." He sighed. "Come on, then." Nate gave her a small, quick kiss.

Chapter Eighteen

His parents' home was even more lovely inside. They stood in the foyer, which was quite large, but they still weren't into the house yet. He took her coat and hung it in the closet. Then he opened the door into the house. A stunning staircase greeted them, with a sitting room to the right and a fireplace with a cozy, crackling fire in the living room to the left. The smell in the home was divine; it felt so warm and welcoming. His mom greeted them.

"Hey, Nathan, it's so good to see you." She had her arms around him. She was so pretty and tall, with dark brown hair with streaks of gray. He had his mom's eyes, and it was striking how much he looked like her.

"Hey, Mom." He smiled.

He loved his mom, and it was all over his face.

"And this must be the lovely Amina."

Before she knew it, she was wrapped up in a hug. It had been years since a mom had hugged her. She missed it.

"Is that my son I hear?" Nate's dad walked into the foyer. Just as tall as he was, just as handsome—the same fluffy hair, strong build, and sharp angles across his face. If you combined the two of them, of course, the outcome would be Nathan. They all were fantastic.

"Hey, Dad, how you doing?" He hugged his father, and she felt all the love.

"And this must be the lovely lady you're seeing. How are you?" He gave Amina a big hug.

She was so grateful for the warm welcome. Nate didn't seem as nervous as he did in the car. He seemed much more relaxed.

"Nathan, please take Amina and show her around the house while we finish getting everything ready," his mom said to him.

"Did you need help with anything?" Amina asked.

"Oh, no, sweetheart, we got it, go see the house. We'll call you guys when it's time to eat."

The living room was decorated with big couches and chairs positioned in front of panoramic windows. The backdrop for the backyard was the lake. A lit gazebo settled on a perfectly manicured lawn. Amina was speechless. He also showed her the gourmet kitchen where his parents were hard at work, his dad's office, the den, and then he took her upstairs.

"You grew up in this house?" she asked as they walked around upstairs. She was a bit overwhelmed.

"Yes, this is it. A bit much for the three of us. A family trying to move into this neighborhood now would probably have to sacrifice their firstborn. It wasn't like that back then. My dad always tells me that."

"What does he do?" she asked.

"He owns a construction company, and my mom teaches at Northwestern. This is my old room here. My mom refused to convert it into an office like my dad wanted when I never moved back home." He laughed. "She eventually took the posters and stickers off the wall."

"I would've loved to have seen what was on your walls." Amina laughed as she walked into his old bedroom.

It was larger than she expected. Clean and neat, and somehow, it smelled like him. She walked over to the window, and there was another remarkable view of the lake from his room. Considering where his dad's office was, she knew why he wanted this room.

"It wasn't what you think. I was such a nerdy kid. It was all about *Star Wars*, Dungeons & Dragons, *Lord of the Rings*, video games. It still is, I guess." He laughed. "I mean, I liked basketball, but that came later, as I got taller."

Amina sat down on the bed. "You sound so much like David."

"I know. I relate to him a lot." He smiled.

"No neighborhood girlfriends you were trying to spy on from the window?"

He sat down next to her. "Nope. Girls didn't come on my radar until I was like in the ninth grade."

"Oh, wow, you were a late bloomer. I remember having

my first crush on a boy when I was in the sixth grade."

"They just weren't on my mind. I was oblivious."

"Too busy plotting which Usher song you would sing to them?" She giggled.

"I cannot confirm or deny." He laughed and swayed his body toward her.

"I'm sure many girls were trying to get your attention. You've always had this face, right?" She leaned into him and kissed him on the cheek.

"My friends would always tell me about girls liking me, but I didn't care. When I got to high school, though—a totally different story."

"The blinders were way off by then, huh." Amina pushed her shoulder against his.

"Glad they were. Glad I saw you." He kissed her.

She pulled away and stroked his bottom lip with her thumb. "I'm glad too," she said as his hands wandered underneath her skirt.

"Dr. Nathan Moore, I know damn well you are not trying to do this with your parents moments away from telling us Thanksgiving dinner is ready," she whispered.

"I am," he whispered in her ear. He got up, moved to the door, and locked it. He turned and grinned in the way she loved. "We're both adults, and they expect us to steal kisses here and there, so that explains your lipstick."

"Yes, that explains that, but there's always an after-sex look. How will that be explained?"

"We'll have to figure that out. But they waste a lot of time talking, and she's always correcting him on something. I give it at least another forty-five minutes until she calls us, which is plenty of time. You have to try to be quiet." He kneeled in front of her.

"I can't make any promises," she whispered. She wanted him too—the excitement of being with him coursed through her veins.

"I need you to do something for me. Just one thing, and I'll do the rest."

"Anything."

"Take off your skirt."

Amina did what he wanted and sat back down on the bed. He put his hand on her face and kissed her in a way that set her on fire. His fingers found her, and her breath caught.

"You feel so good, Amina," he whispered in her ear.

She bit her lip. She was already ready to explode. Nate made her feel so sexy and alive.

Amina lay back while Nate kneeled in front of her. He wrapped her legs around his shoulders and kissed her center, moving his mouth slowly. He teased her, and then he began to feast on her. She grabbed Nate's head and pushed her hips around him, and bit her lip to keep quiet. He felt so good. They needed to be quick, but she didn't want to be. She didn't want him to stop. He moaned in delight, and she put her fist in her mouth, but it was just too good.

They were trying to pull themselves together in the bathroom when his mom called them down for dinner.

Amina laughed and whispered, "She has to know. She has to know her sweet son was upstairs getting it on. It's like she set a timer."

"Please don't say these things." Nate clearly was not amused. "How do I look?" he asked.

"That sex look. You can't fake it." She laughed.

"Come on, let's go downstairs and see what list of questions she has ready for you."

"MRS. MOORE, WHAT do you teach at Northwestern?" Amina asked as she placed a napkin in her lap.

The quiet was making her anxious and causing her mind to wander about what they could be thinking of her. She, of course, wanted to make a good impression.

"I teach interpersonal relationships."

"I had a course similar to that in college. There was a heated discussion around race and feminism. Everyone is always a feminist until you start getting into how race affects women very differently," Amina said.

"Oh, yes! That is so true, and it's something that is frequently overlooked. It leads to questions of who is a true feminist. How can you call yourself one if you won't acknowledge that a Black woman's experience is not the same as a white woman's? To deny that, by in large, I don't think could make her a true feminist."

"Indeed. I remember there was a Caucasian girl in my class who couldn't quite understand that even though we're both women, our lives would never be the same. That it's double the work for Black women."

"Oh my, yes, it's a very difficult thing for some women to reconcile that you have twice as many hoops to jump through. Such a great point. We're going to be getting into all of that after the break. Nathan, can she come to class with me?" She laughed.

Amina was grateful that his mother understood what life must be like for her on a daily basis. They seemed to be making a connection, and they saw things in the same way.

During the rest of the dinner, Nate's parents asked all the usual questions. Where she grew up, what school she went to, and she, of course, teased them about being Wildcats. She talked to them about her father and his health and how he had raised her and Amir. She was sad to leave for Amir's; it would be nothing like this, not warm and inviting and relaxed.

Was she ready to deal with whatever bullshit her brother had up his sleeve?

AMIR'S HOUSE WAS a beautiful single-family home nestled into the neighborhood. The front porch was very inviting. Nate pulled in front of the house and parked his car. Maybe he was overreacting and everything would be fine.

He held her hand. "Are you sure you're up for this? We can just go home or wait in line at some store for Black Friday. We don't have to do this."

Amina put her hand on his face and rubbed his beard. "It's fine. If anything gets too hot or he steps too far out of line, I'll handle it. Please don't think you have to have a pissing contest with him. That's what he's going to want. Don't give him the satisfaction."

Nate grinned.

"I'm not joking. Please, for me."

"Okay." He kissed her forehead.

They waited on the front porch for someone to answer. Cheryl welcomed them with a warm smile as she opened the door.

"Mina! It's so good to see you! Thank you so much for coming." She glanced at Nate. "And who is this handsome man next to you?"

"This is Dr. Nathan Moore, my boyfriend. This is my sister-in-law, Cheryl."

She hugged Nate, nice and tight as if she'd known him for years. "Thanks so much for coming. I hope you enjoy yourself tonight."

"Thanks so much for having me." He already liked her. If everyone was like Cheryl, things would be beautiful.

"Come on. Everyone is in the dining room."

"And who is everyone?" Amina stopped with her hands up.

"Amir, the kids, Dad, and Marcus and his wife. The usuals."

Amina looked to heavens.

The house smelled terrific. It was beautifully decorated with art from up and coming African-American artists, and tons of pictures of family adorned the walls.

They followed Cheryl down the hall, past the stairwell, and the living room. Nate stopped at one of the photos on the wall.

"Babe, is that you?" he asked.

"Yep, that's me. Prom. Angela set me up with one of Matt's friends. Mir only has this picture up because he looks good in it. That's a direct quote from him, by the way."

"Well, you look beautiful. If I knew you then, I totally would've asked you out. Those boys were stupid." He kissed her on the cheek.

"High school sweethearts?" She rested her head on his shoulder.

"For sure." He placed his head on hers to calm her nerves a bit.

He could tell by the way she held his hand that she was still on edge.

"Be strong, babe," he whispered as they continued to follow Cheryl.

When they walked into the dining room, every eye turned to them.

"Look who was at the door," Cheryl said.

"Hey, everybody—happy Thanksgiving." Amina waved to the room.

"Auntie Mina!" Two kids ran toward her.

"Guys, this is Dr. Nathan. Can you say hi?"

"Hi, Dr. Nathan. Nice to meet you."

"Hey, guys, nice to meet you too."

"What's up, Nathan?" Marcus reached out his hand and shook Nate's hand.

"Hey, happy Thanksgiving." He couldn't understand why Amina was so on edge. Everything so far was cool.

Amina took a deep breath, took Nate's hand, and walked him to her dad. "Hey, Daddy." She reached down and hugged him. "How are you feeling?"

"I feel good, ready to eat," he said. "So, is this the doctor?" He steeled his glance at Nate.

"Yes, this is Dr. Nathan Moore."

"Hello, Mr. Wright. It's very nice to meet you." He stood strong and firm in front of her father.

"Grab a seat, son." He pointed to the seat next to him.

"Hey, Amir," Amina begrudgingly spoke to her brother, who sat on the other side of the table.

"I don't get a grand introduction?" he asked, irritated. "I'm Amir, her brother."

"Hi. Nathan. It's nice to meet you." He put his hand out for Amir to shake, but he didn't. This must be the bullshit Amina was afraid of.

Nate took the seat next to Amina.

"Hey, Dr. Nathan, do you play video games?" one of the kids asked.

"I sure do. Love them."

"Can you play with us? Mom said the food is going to take at least another twenty minutes, and she doesn't want us in here messing up the room, and no one else is going to come."

He was thrilled to let them pull him out of the hot seat. Especially since Amir was going to make a point of being a jerk to him.

"Mr. Wright, would you mind if I leave to play with your grandkids?"

"By all means."

He let the kids lead him down the hall to the den.

"SO, NATHAN, MINA said you're one of those doctors that put people to sleep?" her father asked as they passed the turkey.

He chuckled. "Yes, sir, I am."

Amir rolled his eyes from across the table.

"You have a problem with him taking care of kids, Mir?" Amina was annoyed; if he wanted to sling the bullshit, she was ready for battle.

"I have a problem with doctors charging so much money to families for care."

"Well, don't get mad at this young man," her dad said.

"He has a job to do. These kids need more young men in the hospital, ready to take care of them. He's not sitting at their bedside with a notepad ready to give them a bill. That seems unfair, Amir." He might be weak, but his tone was sharp and clear.

"Whatever. I know everyone's so happy that Amina finally got a man and all, but I mean, she could've at least found a Black one. There's plenty out there. Don't you think Black women have it hard enough? Then you go and make it harder on yourself by being with him."

Amina felt a hot burn in her chest. Every betrayal she imagined when she walked in with Nate was laid bare in front of her from her brother. She was incensed he said such a thing in front of everyone, but how many other people felt this way when they walked into a room? She tried to breathe easy, but the dagger in chest from him was painful.

"You're out of line, Amir! You need to calm down," her father said.

Amina saw the shift of Nate's body as he leaned in, ready to either launch himself into a verbal diatribe at Amir or jump across the table and wrap his hands around his throat. Amina grabbed his hand very gently and tried to smile at him. *Don't give in to what he wants. Let me handle it.* He leaned back in his chair and relaxed. She took a deep breath. Nate had no idea what she was about to do. She took another deep breath and finally found her words.

"Amir, let me get this straight. You're so worried about

the state of Black women, except the Black woman sitting across from you, who is your flesh and blood. You wanted her to stay in a relationship with a man who was abusing her. Hitting her. Emotionally and verbally abused her. Tried to rape her."

Nate placed his hand on Amina's knee, but she moved it away from him.

Amina continued, "You then turn around and defend that abuser to me and try to make me feel guilty for leaving him." Her dad grabbed her hand as her voice broke. "Even after he broke into my home and stalked me, you're still not standing up for me. Then you have the gall to sit here and tell me about how Black women have it hard. If you don't shut the hell up, Amir...

"Nathan doesn't do any of those things Omar did, so let's just start there. He's a good man. And number two...you know what? I don't need to give you a list. Because honestly, Amir, you don't deserve to hear why, and I don't owe you shit! You should've just sat there and not said a damn thing to me! Don't you ever disrespect my man like that or me again!"

There was so much more she wanted to say, but she stopped herself. Hopefully, he was done being an ass. Her dad squeezed her hand. Although she was disappointed that all of this came out with her niece and nephew in the room, she had to stand up for herself, and Nate didn't deserve to be treated this way. Nate tried to hold her hand, but she quickly let it go.

After Amina and Amir's argument, her dad told a few jokes and Nate shared a few hospital stories that Amina had heard before, but they were hilarious. Even though everyone was smiling, the damage Amir had inflicted was done. Once everyone was done eating, the kids were eager for more video games with Nate. He gave Amina a quick kiss on the cheek and left the room. Amina offered to help Cheryl clean the table, but she insisted Amina spend time with her dad.

"Daddy, I'm sorry that happened at dinner," she said.

"I'm proud of you, Mina," he told her. "He deserved it. His arrogance deserved what it got today. I try to talk to him about how he's treating you. I know that Cheryl has too. He's just not getting it." Her dad looked so disappointed and sad.

"Omar was not a good man or a good person. He was at one point, but he changed. He hurt me in the worst ways possible. I think it just hurts that Amir can't see that. And then for him to say that about me being with Nathan. Is that how you all view me? Is that what everyone thinks when we're together?" Amina put her head in her hands, exhausted.

She didn't want to be dealing with any of this tonight. Everything was going so well, and now it was filled with hurt.

"Mina, you shouldn't feel bad for standing up for yourself. Your niece needs to see you being strong like that. She adores you, and she will remember that moment of her auntie Mina. But no matter what Amir or anyone else thinks, if you are happy with that young man, then you need to be happy. Don't let people steal your joy."

He was right, but she just didn't know if she was strong enough for what was out there. Amir's words cut her deep, and it exposed all of her feelings that were just beneath the surface.

"You know, Mina, I like him. I saw him get ready to jump across the table, then sit back and let you take the lead. That's tough for a man to do. Especially for a big guy like him. I'm sure his ego is huge since he's a doctor."

"You have no idea, Daddy." She gave a small smile.

"I can tell how much he cares about you and respects you. He cares about how you feel, and he listens to you. Don't throw that away because you are so worried about not living up to what people think and you're not with who they think you should be with. It's foolish." He held her hands tightly and looked in her eyes. He kissed her cheek.

"WELL, THAT WAS exhausting," Amina said when they were finally in the car.

"You know, despite everything, I had a good time." Nate grinned.

Amina ignored him as she stared out the window. She had no idea how to handle her relationship with Nate going forward. Was every dinner going to be like tonight when she brought Nathan around? She didn't want to have a screaming match with Amir all the time. He might not have approved of Nathan and the two them dating, but she didn't expect this kind of blowup.

"Babe, are you gonna be okay?"

Amina sighed. "I'm just glad to be going home." Thank goodness he took the hint.

He let Björk play the rest of the ride home and didn't say another word. When they got back, they both were exhausted.

He took off her coat and kissed her. "Just head on up. I'll join you in a few minutes."

She kissed him on the cheek and headed upstairs, where she undressed, put on her pajamas, went into the bathroom and washed the makeup off her face, and climbed into bed.

How could she make things better with Amir? Maybe she could have them hang out and talk? Maybe she could try to talk to him alone about everything that happened tonight? She leaned her head against the headboard, tossing ideas around in her head of how to fix this mess.

Nathan's arrival broke her train of thought. He stopped at the foot of the bed and took off his clothes. She wasn't ready to say goodbye to what stood before her, but she had to be honest with him about how she felt. He climbed into bed and tried to pull Amina to his chest, but she didn't move.

"Amina, please tell me that you're not letting what your brother said bother you." Nate sighed.

"I'm sorry that I have those concerns and worries. I don't have the privilege of seeing the world the way you do. You don't have the burdens I have, Nathan. Even your mom seems to understand that."

"Listen, I know the world looks very different for us. But you're acting like we are the first interracial couple in the entire world."

"No, the world looks very different for me. Plus, we have no idea what those couples have gone through and what they face on the day-to-day basis. Nate, my job is literally having athletes go into Black communities to help them with various needs. Do you remember when we went out a few weeks ago to dinner? How uncomfortable I felt? One of the players was at the restaurant. He stared at us the entire time. Who knows what he went back and told the other players on the team, or other people I work with in the office. It probably feels like such a slap in the face to them. They must be thinking I pretend to care so much, but here I am with you."

Nate rubbed his beard, tossed the covers back, and got out of the bed. "Amina, why does it matter to you so much?"

"Because I've prided myself on being Black and loving my people and, being with you, it just seems like I'm turning my back on them. Plus, I mean Amir's not wrong, it will make my life harder. How can you not see that, when so many others do?"

"Amina, I do see that, and I understand how you feel. I don't want you to think that I don't. But I've told you time and time again that we can face it all together, and, honestly, I don't know what more I can say or do at this point. It seems like you care more about what anyone else says over what I have to say. I care about you and want to be with you more than anything. I wish that was enough for you."

Nate sat down on his side of the bed. He turned away from her, dejected, as he turned the light off on bedside table. Amina wanted to reach out and comfort him for all of the hurtful words she'd said, but it wouldn't make any difference. She lay down on her side of the bed, and quietly cried herself to sleep.

Chapter Nineteen

A PHONE CALL from the hospital woke Nate up the day after Thanksgiving. The doctor on call was sick, and they couldn't get anyone else. He was still so upset and shaken from everything that happened with Amina, the break from her was right on time.

"Amina, could you drive me to the hospital? You can wait for me at the loft, and when I'm done, we can drive back here."

"Sounds good. It looks like it's snowing. When we get to the loft, can we walk over to the hospital?"

"I'd really like that. You know, when I'm done with everything today, I would like for us to talk." Hopefully, things would get better.

They arrived at the hospital, which was Amina's first time there. She held Nate's hand as they walked through the hallways. At every turn, nurses huddled up. They waved and smiled at him, with little care that Amina stood next to him. Did he have to deal with that on the day-to-day basis? Yet he said good morning to every one of them. She prided herself on not being jealous and understood that Nate was hot, so women would stare, but this was unnerving. He introduced her to various doctors, nurses, and executives. All of them were so kind and had nothing but sweet things to say about him.

They finally reached his office where she noticed a security guard located near his door. The guard tried not to be visible, but she knew that wasn't a regular location, and he was only there as a result of Omar. She'd brought this to Nathan at a children's hospital. Was this the reason why those nurses were all huddled up together? Did they know who she was and what had happened because he was with her?

She felt sick. On top of everything else, this was further confirmation of how difficult things would be for them. She walked into his office, went to the couch, and sat down. Would he be better off with one of those women who were staring at him? All she would ever want is for him to be happy and safe. Without any judgment or embarrassment. His life would be less complicated if he were with someone else.

"Are you okay, babe?" he asked.

"Security guard? A result of Omar?" she asked. "I'm so sorry that I brought this to your job and put your career in jeopardy. I saw all the nurses huddled, whispering when we walked by. I can't imagine what is said about you around this place."

"Stop it, please stop," he whispered. He sat down next to Amina and put his arm around her. "You didn't make him come here and do that. He did that all on his own. You didn't make him make these stupid choices. I don't give a shit about anything anybody says about me. Let them talk. I know who I am, whatever they say or think means nothing. I wish you would deal with things that way. Screw them and anyone else who has a problem with us being together for any reason. None of it matters."

She'd been waiting for the other shoe to drop, and it did. So much of her life had been surrounded by drama, and he didn't need any of it. He didn't need to deal with her ex being a stalker and all of the other shit that came along with being with someone Black. He deserved better.

"Nate, I'm just not the right person for you." Amina's voice steeled as she realized what needed to be done.

"Amina, you are exactly right for me. I wish you could see that. I can't believe you are letting everyone around us ruin something that has been so amazing."

"Nate—"

She was interrupted by Shawn walking through the door.

"Hey, Amina, how are you?"

She stood and tried to keep her emotions in check. "Hey, Shawn, it's good to see you. How are you?"

"Good. Sorry to interrupt but your man and I have a surgery we have to get to."

Nate stood with a blank look on his face.

"Shawn, can you give us a minute? I'll meet you in a few. I won't be late."

"Sure. Good to see you, Amina."

But she didn't know what to say after the door closed. Nate took her hands and placed them against his chest.

"Amina, please know how much I care about you. I fully accept you for who you are, baggage and all. I am willing to fight through anything for you, and with you. I hate I have to leave you with so much we need to talk about, but I have to go."

She ran her fingers across his shirt while he spoke and made sure she memorized how his chest felt.

"Please wait for me at the loft, and we can talk about everything tonight. Please. Please don't give up on us."

She hugged him and held him as tightly as she could. She pulled away, and he held her face in his hands, kissed her, and left his office.

She aimlessly wandered the snowy Chicago streets. Her magical ride with Nate had come to an end. She'd seen the remnants of what she brought into his life. It was too much. Maybe he'd end up with one of the nurses, a sweet, kind woman. He wouldn't have to deal with stares and whispers from being with her.

Nate was so good, and he deserved the best.

When she made it back to the loft, every surface held a memory. Everywhere they'd made love and all the laughter they shared. She went upstairs and remembered their first night together as she sat on the bed. Her entire body ached from already missing him. She knew this would be painful, but she was doing the right thing by letting him go.

She put all of her thoughts into a letter and placed it on the bed. She cried her way out of the loft to Angela's.

Chapter Twenty

NATE LEFT THE hospital after his last surgery as quickly as he could. He couldn't believe Amina was letting the world around them ruin their relationship. She was everything, and he was going to do all he could to make her see that she was.

But when he opened the door to his loft, all of the lights were off, and he knew. It felt so cold and lonely inside as he walked around. He called her name but knew she wouldn't answer. He walked upstairs and hoped to see her stretched out on the bed taking a nap. But there was nothing, only the hint of her smell still in the room.

He sat down on the bed next to the letter she left. He didn't want to read it, but he had to know what led her to leave him. All of it was wrong, every word of it. He didn't know what to do to make her see. She was so crazy to think she needed to leave. All of his worst fears had come true. How could he have been so wrong? He couldn't call to talk to her—she very clearly had asked him not to.

Instead, he called Chris and Shawn to come over, went

downstairs, grabbed a beer out of the fridge, and sat on the couch.

"What the hell happened?" Chris asked.

Nate didn't say a word and handed them the letter Amina left.

"Damn," Shawn said after he read her letter.

"So, what are you going to do?" Chris asked.

"I mean, what can I do? Nothing. Being with me freaked her out, and she ran away. It's done." He tossed the letter across the room.

"You didn't scare her away, man. She laid it all out. All the trauma from her past, all of the challenges you would face together, all of her doubts. It was all too much. She feels like you guys would end up not making it because of all of the mess. She wants you to be drama free, and that means her walking away. Nothing is your fault," Shawn said to his friend.

"I get that," Nate said. "I'm just not sure why she couldn't wait until I got home to talk to me. So we can work through how she was feeling. I don't understand why she would give up on us, on me."

"Do you honestly think we would be here if she felt like she could tell you this face-to-face? Amina needed to be as honest with you as she could, and this was the best way she could do that. Probably talking to you would've been too hard because of how much she cares about you, bro."

Nate sat back on his couch and stared at the ceiling. "I

have no idea what I'm supposed to do now. How do I just move on? I've found the woman I am supposed to be with. Her walking away isn't going to change that."

A WEEK AFTER she'd left the loft, Detective Ross called her to let her know the details of Omar's release, and she handled that news surprising well. He was admitted to a psych clinic for in-house treatment for possible bipolar disorder. Amina was relieved that Omar would be getting some much-needed help. She called Amir when she got the news about the bond release and the conditions.

"Hey, Mina, I heard the news."

"Yeah, you were right along." She sighed.

"I don't take any pleasure in that, believe me. I'm sorry I can't talk right now. I'm swimming in a cases. But we'll talk later about it all. How are you doing?"

"Not good. Wondering if he'll get better. Wondering if I did the right thing with Nathan. The one bright spot is work is going really well."

"Be strong, sis. I know that I haven't been the best for you. I know that. Despite all of that, I love you, okay? Hang in there."

"Love you too, Mir."

Hopefully, Omar would get the help he needed, and he would no longer feel the need to be a part of her life. Maybe he would finally let her go.

Over the next few days and weeks, she spent a lot of time with her dad, whose health started to decline significantly. But she missed Nate and wished he was there when she came home from her visits with her father. He knew exactly what to say, how to make her laugh, and comfort her.

The week of Christmas came, and she and Amir always spent that time with their dad. Ever since he'd gotten sick, they kept the tradition of waking up on Christmas morning together, just the three of them.

"Mina, thanks for catering everything for us. It was delicious."

"No problem. I just wasn't up for cooking."

"Have you spoken to the doctor at all, sweetheart?" her dad asked.

"No, and I don't plan on it. It's all for the best."

"Be a shame for you to let go of all that joy and happiness for something silly like other people's thoughts and opinions."

Amina didn't say a word. She pushed through every day and tried to focus on the fact that she'd done the right thing.

"Hey, Dad, let me get you to bed," Amir said.

"Good night, sweetheart." Dad gave her a kiss on the forehead.

"Night, Daddy, see you in the morning."

Amir returned to the living room and sat down on the couch next to her. He elbowed her and smiled.

"Thanks, Mir, for taking care of Dad and for stopping

where that conversation was going."

"No problem. I could see you were having a hard time talking about Nate. What happened anyway? I mean, if you're up to talking about it."

"I don't mind. Long story short, it was so much drama. I didn't think he deserved to deal with it." She paused. "Mir, they put a security guard by his office because of Omar. I just felt like I was ruining his rep, you know?"

He sighed. "Mina, I haven't been there for you lately, and things haven't been great."

"No, they haven't. There was a time in our lives when we were much closer."

"I know I've played a huge role in that. I've been going through a lot with my job, my marriage, the kids. It all became so much, and I didn't know how to handle things. I'm sorry for how I treated you and for being a part of the drama. I've been seeing a therapist to help me get things back on track, and it's been constructive. One of the things that I've come to realize is I wasn't fair to you or to Nathan. Most of all, I'm sorry for Omar. Even though I thought something was wrong, you should've been my priority. I hope you can forgive me for that."

Amina hugged her brother. She had been waiting for so long to hear those words from him. She needed him more than ever.

"Mina, I only met Nathan once, and I saw how much he loved you. He was willing to kick my ass without a second thought. It seemed like he wanted to be by your side through anything. You deserve to be happy, and it looked like he made you incredibly happy."

"I'm just scared, Mir. He's so good. I want to be strong and not care about what other people think, but it's hard."

"You had no problem telling my ass off." He laughed.

"Well, you're you. I can't do that to every stranger on the street. Or feel like I have to."

"Sis, you have to decide just how much he's worth to you. What are you willing to deal with? You're walking around with this sad face. He means something, otherwise you wouldn't be giving any of this a second thought. If you get a chance, you have to try to give it another shot and have a little faith in how much you mean to each other. Be brave."

She smiled at him and couldn't believe those words came from his mouth. "I see all that therapy is working on you."

They laughed together and stayed up all night and talked, something she'd really missed doing.

ANGELA STROLLED INTO the house a few weeks after the holiday. Amina was on the couch buried under her favorite blanket.

Angela sighed. "Mina, I love you, and that means I have to give it to you straight. Nathan clearly is in love with you. I'm not sure how you've missed that, but I noticed it weeks ago. He was willing to be by your side through any struggles or challenges you faced. No matter what they were. He didn't care what they were. You are one of the smartest people I know, but you're being really stupid right now."

"Hey." Amina frowned.

"Well, you are. Nathan loves you, he respects you, and has done nothing to trigger this reaction."

"Angie, it's just… Do you know how terrible it feels to be in a coffeeshop, standing in line holding the hand of this kind and sweet man, and whispers surround you? Black women shaking their heads as they'd look at us. And let's not even get into the family drama with Amir. None of that nastiness would've happened if we weren't together." Amina was resolute that all of this was for the best, no matter how much she missed Nate. Deep down, she knew he was the one, but she was afraid of what that meant.

"Mina, you are putting way too much pressure on yourself for no reason. Because there's a few assholes out there that won't be happy. So what! Are you happy? I've seen you with him, and your face lights up whenever he's around. Come on, Mina. Think!

"You've had enough moping around. You're going out tonight. It's time to go out, have some fun, and have a few drinks. Go upstairs and get dressed. Let's go."

Amina wanted to protest and stay hidden in her house, but Angela would throw her on the bed and dress her like a toy doll, so she went upstairs and got ready. She kept it as simple as possible. Jeans, T-shirt, scarf, hair down, and a little bit of makeup. They drove downtown, went into some bar, and met up with a few of their other girlfriends she hadn't seen for some time.

"Hey, Mina! I have missed you!" Lisa said. "Angela filled me in on everything. I know it's hard. Just be here, and try to enjoy the night, okay?"

"Okay." Amina sighed.

She was a little happy to be out of the house. She had been so consumed with trying not to think about him, she forgot how to have some fun. Amina laughed and joked around with her girlfriends. This was precisely what she needed.

"I'm going to go over to the bar and grab another drink," she told her friends.

"Okay, girl, don't get lost."

Amina got to the bar, and she heard a song— "Hunnybee" by Unknown Mortal Orchestra; a song she'd put on a playlist for Nate. She smiled and sang along to it for a bit. She ordered a drink and nodded her head to the song. When she looked across to the other side of the bar, Nate's eyes pierced right through her. Amina completely froze and couldn't hear a sound.

His handsome face stared back at her, and he looked fantastic. His hair was very short, and he wore a Henley underneath some kind of blue coat. She knew it was blue because the blue in his eyes shined bright. She had no idea what to do, so she just stood there and watched him. For a moment, she thought Angela had set her up, but when the bartender came back with her drink and broke their eye contact, she looked across the bar to see if he was still there, but he was gone. Even if she could just stare at him and say nothing, it was better than not seeing him at all.

She turned to go back to her friends, and there he was.

Chapter Twenty-One

S HE WAS JUST as beautiful as always. When Chris and Shawn made him leave his loft after he buried himself in his work, the gym, and video games, Nate never expected he would run into the woman he was still so crazy about. He thought about her every second of every day they had been apart. His parents asked about her every day, implored him to call her or to visit. One day, he was a block away from her house before he turned around. He didn't want to be a creep, and he wanted to respect what she wanted. He missed Amina, and all he wanted was for her to be in his life, to build a future with her. But he had no idea how to make her understand that she didn't need to be afraid of them failing, and she was more than enough for him. She was all he needed or wanted. More than anything, he was happy she was standing in front of him.

"How are you?" He leaned down and spoke close to her ear.

She smelled like sunshine.

"Pretty good." She nodded.

He smiled. "Can we go and talk somewhere a little quieter? Please?"

"Yes, I would like that."

He took her hand and tried to find a table in a lounge area farther in the back of the bar away from everyone. Amina took out her phone to let Angela know where she was. Grizzly Bear's "Three Rings" played, and Nate knew the song.

He smiled at the memory. "Such a good song."

"My dad asked about you over the holiday."

"How is your dad?"

"He's not doing too well. His health has taken a turn for the worst. He's bedridden now. It's been a tough few weeks. Pretty sure this was our last Christmas with him."

Nate reached out for her hand but wasn't sure if he should. He didn't know if she would take it or what message it would send. He needed to know where she stood. They sat, unsure of what to say to each other.

"So, did your friends drag you out of your house too?" He laughed and hoped to break through the thickness in the air.

"Angela's exact words were, 'it's time to stop moping around the house and get out of here.'" Amina laughed. "Honestly, I've been pretty down. I've missed you, Nathan."

He reached across the table, took her hand, and kissed it. He smiled at her. "You have no idea how much I have missed you, Amina."

Her shoulders relaxed. Nate reached out and pulled her into his arms. Amina took a deep breath, and he sat back down across from her.

"Do you want to stay here, or do you want to leave and go somewhere else to talk?" he asked.

They went to his loft, which was a bit of a mess. He was always so organized, but there were shoes everywhere, and clothes hung on the back of the chairs in the dining room.

"Can we talk about all of this now, please?" he asked. She nodded. "What happened?"

"I went into a panic over everything. Seeing the way all those women were looking at you, then seeing the security guard by your office. What Amir said on Thanksgiving. It was all so much at once. Nate, you're such a good man, and it felt like you deserved more than this situation," she whispered.

"Why wouldn't you wait to talk to me about all of this when I got home?" He was frustrated. "Amina, you didn't have any faith in us at all. You didn't have any faith in me or my feelings for you. You assumed I wouldn't understand how you felt and what you were going through. When I tell you I'm all in and I accept you for who you are, you don't believe me. Why? Why is it so hard for you to understand that what I tell you, I mean it. You didn't even consider how coming home and finding you gone would impact me. That letter was crushing. It was a shitty way for me to find out how you felt. I couldn't believe you would do that to me. I thought we were better than that."

She sat in silence and sighed. "Nathan, I'm sorry I didn't handle things in the best way. I'm sorry that I didn't have enough faith in us, in you, to trust in you. I'm truly sorry for that." He wouldn't look at her, but he listened. "I was foolish and selfish to not think about you and how what I was doing would hurt you—the effects of all of my drama."

Nate got on his knees in front of her and lifted her chin to meet his eyes. "Amina, I want to be with you. I have never stopped wanting to be with you. Even after I read your letter. I was devastated, but my feelings for you have never changed. You are everything to me. I want you to know that you're enough for me. You have always been enough for me."

"I thought you would hate me."

He put his hands on her face. "Amina, I care about you too much to ever hate you."

"I've missed you so much." She put her hand on his chest, over his heart.

"Babe, you're here now, and we're talking. This is what needed to happen in the first place. You have to talk to me." He folded her in his arms, and she sniffled into his chest. "I know sometimes I can make a joke out of the important stuff, but I listen, and I understand."

"I know."

He held her tighter as they sat on the couch in silence.

"Nate, it's late, and I need to get home."

He felt a sudden sadness. "I can drive you home. I don't mind."

"Thanks."

The drive was a long and quiet one to her house. He pulled into her driveway and smiled when he saw her home. He didn't think he would ever see it or her again. He opened her car door, held her hand, walked her to the door, and inside the house.

"Thanks for driving me home. I appreciate it. It was good seeing you tonight."

He didn't like the tone of her voice. It sounded like she was on the verge of saying goodbye to him for good.

She walked over to him and stood in front of him with her hands on his chest. "Nate, I've missed you every moment since I left your loft. I want to be with you with everything in me. I can't keep running away from how I feel."

He gently placed his hand on her face and stroked her cheek with his thumb and then across her lips. He leaned down and kissed her slowly while she clenched his shirt in her hands. She put her hands in his hair as he moved her against the wall. He kissed her hard and ran his hands all over her body.

He picked her up and carried her upstairs. When they got to the bedroom, he slowed down. He gazed into her eyes as he removed her shirt, and kissed her while he massaged her breasts. He moved and unzipped her jeans and helped her out of them. He kissed her and felt the center of her and loved how good she felt.

Amina lifted his shirt and smiled when she saw his bare chest. She kissed it, moved her hands to unbutton his jeans, and stroked him when he was out of them. When he finally laid her down on the bed, he placed himself in her and slowly made love to her. He would not take it for granted, this moment of having her back. It felt so good to feel her all around him. He made love to her as slowly as his body would allow before they exploded together.

Chapter Twenty-Two

AMINA WOKE UP in the middle of the night and felt his breath on her shoulder, his arm draped around her. She moved closer to him.

He stirred a bit and cleared his throat. "Are you okay?" he asked.

"Yes," she whispered. "You're still here."

He pulled her tighter. "I am."

"I thought it was all a dream." She smiled in the darkness.

"That's a helluva dream."

She felt him smile behind her and the scruff of his beard against her skin, the tingle down her spine she felt whenever it brushed against her.

"Sorry I woke you. I'm not sure if you have to be at the hospital or not."

"I'm not going to work today."

She turned around to face him. "No?"

"Nope." He turned on his back.

"Well then." She climbed on top of him and kissed him.

"Oh, I see what this was all about," he said in between her kisses, and they laughed.

A few hours later, Amina went downstairs and poured herself coffee in the kitchen. She turned on a playlist of all of her favorite indie love songs, sat down at her laptop, and read through her emails. She let him get some much-needed rest. She didn't know how many rounds they went last night.

Her phone rang, and she answered quickly because she didn't want to wake him. It was Angela, probably pissed at how she had disappeared last night.

"I'm happy you're alive," she said.

"Hey, Angie. I'm sorry. I wasn't free to make a call. A lot was happening."

"I don't want to know all of the nasty details, okay?" Angela laughed. "But I'm glad it seems you guys worked it all out."

"Well, we talked." Amina giggled.

"You did more than talk."

"Yes, a few times."

"Damn, still?"

"Got to make up for the lost time." Amina laughed.

"Well, I'm glad you're good. Talk to you later. Love you."

"Love you too." She hung up just as Nate came downstairs.

"Who is it that you love making you laugh like that?" He kissed her on the cheek.

"That was Angela calling to check on me."

He nodded. "Are you okay? Are we okay?" he asked as he poured his coffee. "I'm happy to be here with you. Happy for everything that happened last night. But I know you have some concerns about us, and we need to talk through those things, because in our time apart, I haven't morphed into a Black man." He chuckled.

"No?" Amina smiled.

He sat next to her shirtless, in his boxers, and she worked really hard to maintain a sense of focus.

She put her hand on his face and rubbed his beard. "I have noticed that you haven't magically changed into some melanin-filled person." She kissed his cheek. "Nathan, I know how amazing you are, and how much you care for me too. I struggled with knowing how right you are for me. I fought with my feelings of knowing you could be the one, battling how I was feeling inside and how the outside world would treat us. I'm tired of fighting, babe. I want to see where this goes, and learn how to do this, and fight through it all. Together. I want you, I want us. Can we figure all of this out? Together?"

He kissed her hand, put it down, and held it for a minute. "I want nothing more."

She moved to stand in between his legs and kissed him. She smiled and studied his face when she pulled away.

"Can you stay with me for a few days? I've been away from you for so long, I want to be with you as much as I can."

"Are you sure? You're not going to leave me any more notes, are you?"

"Nope. I'm not going to leave a note or be gone when you come back home. I promise I'm not going anywhere."

He meant the world to her, and she was ready to build a future and life with him. If this was the first step, she needed to take it.

He lifted her chin with the tip of his finger and kissed her slowly. "I'll be here by the end of the night."

She wrapped her arms around him and held him close.

He looked at her when they pulled away from each other. "So, the one, huh?" He laughed.

Amina laughed and pushed him away.

"Guess I got to get to the loft and get packed up. Did you want to come with me?"

"No, I'll stay here and get things cleaned up. I didn't do much over the last few weeks."

"Did you need me to pick up anything while I am out?"

Amina loved how that sentence sounded. "Um, I haven't looked. We'll have to look through everything when you get back."

"Okay, I'm going to jump in the shower. I don't want to be away from you for too long." He kissed her on the cheek and flew up the stairs while she finished cleaning up.

"I should be gone for about an hour or two."

"Okay, I'll be here when you get back."

He kissed her goodbye, and he was out the door.

She immediately called Angela back. "I'm going to have a roommate. At least for a little bit. I just missed him so much. But we're gonna work to figure all of this out, together," she said as she walked upstairs.

"Mina, I am so happy for you and Nathan, I truly am. I don't have time for all the gory details in between meetings. We still on for Saturday brunch?"

"Yes, see you then. Love you, Angie. Thank you for putting up with me for the last few weeks."

"Love you too, Mina, glad it all worked out."

She cleaned a bit more, got some laundry in, and jumped in the shower. While she waited for Nate to come back, she started going through some of her emails. She came across an email from Omar. Amina read and reread the name. He must've gotten her information from Amir. Her brother better not be up to anything shady.

"Mina, hey, how are you?" Amir sounded surprised to hear from her.

"I have some news for you," she said. "I went out with Angela last night and ran into Nathan. We talked and worked things out."

"Oh, yeah? I'm delighted to hear that, Amina. You two seemed happy, so I'm glad you have a second shot at it."

"Thanks, Mir. But did you give my email to Omar?"

"Yes, I gave him your email. His therapist wanted him to reach out to people that he caused great harm. He needs to start making amends. He can't call you or visit you. So the only way he can contact you is through email."

"Technically, that's still a violation." She couldn't yet fully accept what Amir had done.

"Did you read it?" Amir asked.

"Not yet. I wanted to wait to read it with Nathan. Now that I have some background on why I have it that conversation will be easier to have. Have you seen Omar?"

"Yeah, I have. He's doing much better, gained some of the weight back. He sort of had a nervous breakdown before he was officially diagnosed with bipolar disorder. None of that excuses what he did to you, and he's been told that numerous times."

"Does he seem better? Like how he was?"

"He's getting there. It's gonna take some time, but he's definitely on his way back. It's probably good to read it with Nathan. He's probably mentioned him in there too. He feels bad and wants to be better and for you to be free of him. He wants you to be happy."

"Thanks for giving him my email, but don't give him any more of my info. I know he's trying to get better, but I don't want any more attachment to him. I'm finally in a place where I'm healing and happy, and I don't need to be reminded of all of that ugliness."

"Got it."

"All right, gotta run. Love you, Mir."

Nate finally arrived back to the house with a total of four suitcases, two duffel bags, and a carrying case for his PlayStation.

"Hey, babe, sorry it took so long." He walked in and kissed her. "I had to check and double-check I had everything before I left."

"Um, all this for a week?" Amina laughed.

"Hey, the goal is for me to stay, right? Isn't that what we're working toward?" He kissed her and smiled.

She grabbed his duffel bags, and he carried his suitcases upstairs. She tried to make room for him in the closet. She found a corner for him with just enough room for all of the clothes he needed to hang. There was always the closet in the guest bedroom he could use. Both of them were addicted to sneakers, so sharing the space was going to be quite the challenge. She ended up having much more drawer space than closet space, so that helped.

He spent the next hour setting up his PlayStation in her office. Amina would not agree to have him take up the living room space with it. She wasn't compromising on that. She could not stop laughing at the amount of stuff he brought for such a short amount of time. But deep down, she knew he was never leaving.

She sat him down in the living room before dinner with her laptop.

"So, Amir gave Omar my email address, and he sent me a message as part of his therapy. I didn't want to read it until you got back. Is that okay?"

"Sure, thanks for waiting for me. Let's take a look." Nate pulled her on his lap while Amina found the email, and they begin to read.

DEAR AMINA,

I HOPE THAT YOU ARE DOING WELL. I WON'T TAKE UP TOO MUCH OF YOUR TIME. THE DOCTORS THINK IT'S IMPORTANT FOR ME TO MAKE AMENDS TO ALL THE PEOPLE I'VE HURT, AND THERE'S NO ONE I'VE HURT MORE THAN YOU. FOR ALL OF IT, MINA, I'M DEEPLY SORRY. I KNOW THOSE WORDS WON'T DO A WHOLE LOT, BUT I NEEDED YOU TO HEAR THEM FROM ME. YOU WERE THE FIRST WOMAN I LOVED, AND TO KNOW I HURT YOU HURTS ME MORE THAN YOU COULD EVER REALIZE. BY NOW I'M SURE AMIR TOLD YOU ABOUT MY DIAGNOSIS, BUT THAT DOESN'T ERASE THE PAIN THAT I INFLICTED ON YOU.

YOU'VE MOVED ON, AND I'M HAPPY FOR YOU. YOU FOUND A GUY WHO WAS READY TO KICK MY ASS AT THE DROP OF A HAT, WITHOUT A CARE IN THE WORLD FOR THE CONSEQUENCES. AND THAT'S GREAT. I WISH YOU TWO NOTHING BUT THE BEST, AND I HOPE YOU CAN APOLOGIZE TO HIM FOR ME AS WELL. THAT'S ALL. THERE'S REALLY NOTHING MORE TO SAY. I AM GOING TO GET BETTER AND DO MY BEST TO HAVE A GOOD LIFE—HEALTHY AND FREE FROM HURTING OTHERS. I HOPE YOU'LL FORGIVE

ME, AND KNOW NONE OF WHAT HAPPENED WAS EVER YOUR FAULT.

THANKS FOR READING,
OMAR

Amina exhaled a breath she hadn't realized she was holding. Nate kissed her cheek.

"Maybe we can talk to Amir to have some of the charges dropped."

"Yeah, I'd like that," she whispered.

"You gonna be okay?"

"Yeah, let's go." She kissed him and closed her laptop, ready to leave Omar in the past.

For so long, he had a hold on her heart, and now it was gone, finally. She could look toward what was ahead with Nathan free from any lingering fear of Omar ruining any more of her life.

Chapter Twenty-Three

I T WAS THREE a.m. when her phone rang. She looked at the screen and saw that it was Amir.

"Mir, what's wrong?"

"Dad! He stopped breathing. He's at the University of Chicago Hospital. Meet you there."

"Okay, on my way."

"Drive safe."

Amina's heart raced. She jumped out of bed and tried to creep, but he was awake.

"What's wrong?" he asked softly.

"My dad. Amir said he stopped breathing, and I'm meeting him at the hospital." Her voice broke. "You can go back to sleep. I'll let you know what's going on when I get there." She fumbled around in the dark.

Nate put on the lamp, got out of bed, and very calmly started getting dressed.

"What are you doing? You have to be at the hospital in a few hours," she said.

"I'm coming with you. You can't drive over to the south

side like this alone. Someone can cover my shift."

He walked to the bathroom while Amina threw on some clothes.

When he came out, he walked over to her and put his hands on her shoulders. "I'll meet you downstairs." He kissed her on the cheek and her body shook.

She nodded, went into the bathroom, and brushed her teeth. As she stared at herself in the mirror, it hit her that she could lose her father in a matter of hours or minutes, and she broke down. His health was in bad shape and it was only a matter of time. It appeared that time had come.

But how could she face life without him?

When she made it downstairs, she put on her coat, stepped into some sneakers, and climbed into Nate's car. She held his hand as he drove to the hospital, grateful that he ignored her sometimes, and he was there with her. She needed him. They drove in silence while she stared out the window at every building they passed. Tears spilled down her face. Nate occasionally squeezed her hand to comfort her, but she wasn't ready to face what was coming for her at the hospital.

When they arrived at the hospital, bile rose in her throat as they searched to find Amir. The air was thick, and she felt death in her bones. They found her brother in the waiting area, surrounded by hideous brown chairs. The only comfort was the room was empty, and it was just him and Tina. Amina's legs were unsteady and weak the closer she got to him. Amir always looked so put together, calm, arrogant almost. He looked shaken and afraid.

"Hey," she said and hugged him.

"Hey, Mina." He sniffled. "There's been no change right now. He's unconscious, and they're running tests." Nate put his arm around her waist to steady her.

She hugged Tina too. "Thank you for being with him," she said. "If you weren't there, he probably would be gone."

Amina looked back over her shoulder and she saw Amir hugging Nate. For a brief moment, she smiled. Sometimes small wishes and miracles came true. After everything, it was clear that Amir had accepted Nate.

But her father would never see this. He would never have the boys over to hang out with him while he watched a game.

"Did the doctor say anything else?" she asked.

"No. They want to see how long he wasn't breathing and what caused it. We just have to wait."

"You guys sit down. I'm going to go try to find some coffee for everyone," Nate said.

He leaned down and kissed her on the lips briefly. Tina offered to go with him.

"Dad was happy you two got back together, you know. I told him yesterday." Amir punched her shoulder.

"Did you? We were planning on visiting him this weekend. To watch some games with him."

"Yeah. He said, 'Her man came back around again.'"

"He did." She smiled as she sniffled.

"Nate's a good dude. I feel bad for giving him shit, especially seeing him here with you now."

"Well, you have time to make it up to him. He'll be around." Amina elbowed him for a brief moment of happiness.

"Are Cheryl and the kids coming?"

"No. I told her I would call her once I got more info. She was distraught when I left. Worried about how the kids would take the news. But I told her that if she needed to come, I would call her." They sat down on a set of brown chairs.

"Mir, I'm not ready." She put her head on his shoulder and cried.

They sat for a few minutes, alone, just the two of them as heartbreak hung over the room.

"How many Saturdays do you think you've spent watching Michigan games with Dad over the last six years?" he whispered.

"Probably hundreds."

"Yeah. I tried to figure out how many Monday night football games I've watched with him over the last few years. I lost count. Then when you consider the games while we were growing up... So many things he's done." He stopped talking and leaned his head over hers. They sat as tears flowed down their faces.

"I'm not ready either, Mina."

Nate eventually came back with coffee, but she didn't want any. She shifted her head from Amir's shoulder to Nate's. He sat and held her hand while they waited on an update on her father.

"Nate," she whispered. "Thanks for being here."

He kissed her hair. "Of course."

She leaned closer to him, closed her eyes, and inhaled him. She had a bit of ease and comfort with him at her side. Finally, the doctor came out. Amina and Amir stood, grabbed each other's hands, and braced themselves.

"He's awake, but he's not out the woods. Not sure how things are going to go throughout the rest of the night. Cancer has progressed, and it's taking a toll on every part of his body at this point."

"Can we see him?" Amir asked.

"Yes, you guys can see him, but only for a few minutes."

They all went into the hospital room, where her father lay in his bed connected to tons of tubes. The room was dark; the only light was from all of the monitors and the buildings outside. He looked so small and defeated but also at peace. He knew he was at his end. She wished she had some soothing music to play for him, but the sound of beeping machines was going to be the soundtrack for this moment.

"Hey, Daddy." Amina's voice felt so small as it escaped her body.

"Hey, my babies." His voice sounded so weak, raspy, and

tired. "Sorry I scared everyone."

"Daddy, don't apologize." She went and sat next to him, held his hand, and kissed it several times. Amir held his other hand.

"Thank you, Tina, for acting so fast and for calling the ambulance. She saved my life." Tina kissed him on the cheek.

"Oh, I see the doctor is here. Look at all that joy," he whispered.

It broke her heart that he would never see her in a wedding dress or walk her down the aisle. He would never hold their child in his arms.

"It's great to see you two found your way back to each other," Dad continued. "Mir, are Cheryl and the kids on their way?" he asked.

"I can have her bring them."

"Please, go and do that," he said to his son.

Amina's heart sank. He held on just to say goodbye to his grandkids.

Luckily, Amir didn't live that far from the hospital. Cheryl and the kids made it there as fast as they could, the kids still were in their pajamas. The amount of time Amina had with her father slipped away.

This was going to break the entire family. He was the one everyone talked to when they were down, when they needed perspective, or they just needed love and kindness. He gave it to everyone unconditionally with pure delight.

"Mr. Wright, thanks for being so kind to me. I appreciate that you accepted me dating your daughter. I care about her very much. I will do my very best to protect her, to comfort her, and give her joy every day, sir," she overheard Nate murmur.

"I know you will. I will haunt you every day of your life if you don't." He smiled and hugged Nate.

This small moment was a gift for Amina.

"She's going to need you, son. Let her do what she needs to, be patient, and wait on her," he whispered.

"I promise I will, Mr. Wright." Nate's voice quivered.

"Good man, Dr. Moore."

The kids were next to talk to their grandpa, then Nate offered to take them to the lobby and join Tina and Cheryl there. He kissed Amina's cheek, and she held on to him for a moment.

"Do you need me to stay?" he asked.

"No. I want to be alone with him. Just me, him, and Amir."

When the room was quiet, they both sat on either side of him and held a hand.

"Daddy," Amina began, but he squeezed her hand, and she stopped.

"Let me speak." He struggled, and they leaned close to hear him. He got weaker by the second. "When your mom left, I didn't know what the hell I was going to do with you two." He smiled as he looked at them. "The clothes, school, hair, working, homework, girlfriends, boyfriends, sports, graduations, a wedding, grandkids. We made it through it all."

"Yes, we did," Amir said through his tears.

"I'm so happy you two have worked things out. You two need each other. You cannot let the nonsense keep you two apart. It was tough seeing you at odds, so I'm glad that you both could stop being so silly and love each other. It's been my greatest honor being your father, a gift. There's been nothing greater than that; you two are my joy. Sure, there was some bad, some hurt, and some pain along the way. But always a joy. Always my joy. I'll miss you both, but I know I will see you again. Until then, promise me you will hold on to your joy and find more and more of it every day. No matter how small it is, grab hold of it."

"We will, Daddy. We will." Amina could hardly speak.

"We promise," Amir said.

"I love you both, to the stars." They smiled.

He said that to them every night he put them to bed when they were younger.

"To the stars," they whispered at the same time and pointed at the ceiling.

They both leaned down and kissed his forehead.

He smiled, whispered, "I love you," took one last breath, and he was gone.

THE RAIN AGAINST the windows alarmed her. Amina opened her eyes. How did she get home? The clouds mirrored her sorrows, and she felt sick. It was three in the afternoon, and she felt like she had been hit by a truck. The one person who loved her most in the world was gone. She wasn't sure how that pain was ever going to go away. She had no idea how or if she would ever get over this feeling of loneliness. When she heard footsteps coming upstairs, she lay back down and pulled the covers over her head. She didn't want to see anyone.

"Hey, Auntie Mina." David's voice filled the room.

He spoke as softly as an eleven-year-old could. He climbed in bed and put his head on Amina's chest. She pulled the covers back, and he kissed her head.

"Hey, D. Who sent you?" Amina asked, exhausted.

"My mom, Amir, and Nate."

Amina nodded, sat up, and set herself against the headboard as David took a seat next to her.

"How long were they discussing who should come up here before they decided on you?"

"About an hour." He paused. "I'm really sorry about your dad, Auntie Mina," he said with his head against her arm.

"Thanks, D."

"He was always really nice to me. Always made me feel good about myself."

Amina's eyes started to water. She knew this was true

because that was what he had done with her and Amir their whole lives. To know he would no longer be at his apartment, or she would never hear his voice again. It was too much. She took a deep breath. She had to learn how to do this without him.

"So. Catch me up. What's going on? I have no idea when I got home." She wiped a tear away.

"Well, Nate called my mom around six this morning." Of course he called Angie when he stepped out of the room with the kids. She never thought about doing it, and Angela would've wanted to know. Goodness, her mind was blown by his willingness to always to do the right thing for her and make sure she was always taken care of.

"She woke me up and told me, crying. So, we got ready and came straight here. You came home around like eight or nine. I don't remember. You were like, passed out. Nate carried you inside and upstairs, and you've been asleep ever since. He took a quick nap around eleven, woke up, and you were still asleep. He started to get worried. Then Amir texted Nate to see how you were doing. He was telling him about long you were sleeping, so he came over because he was worried. Then my mom said, 'Amir never comes to hipster town.'"

Amina grinned. "She's right. He never comes to the Northside. I think he's been to my house twice. Thanks for the update, D." He was always thorough on details, no matter the subject.

"I think they just want to know you're going to be okay, Auntie. I mean they know you're not okay now, but that you will be. Eventually. I tried to tell them that you would, and just to give you space, but you know, eleven." He laughed and pointed at himself.

"Well, they sent the right person. I wouldn't have gotten up for anyone else." She kissed his forehead.

"I know. I love you, Auntie."

"I love you too, D. Let them know I'll be down shortly."

"Okay." He climbed out of her bed and closed her bedroom door.

Amina sat on her bed, alone, and listened to rain pound against her windows. She didn't know how to move or how to get out of bed. She would typically call her dad and tell him how afraid and abandoned she felt. Amina didn't know how to do this without him. If she stayed here any longer, they would keep sending David up to the room, and she didn't want that to happen.

She put one foot on the floor and took several deep breaths before the other foot followed. She very slowly stood up and gingerly walked into her bathroom to take a shower. She cried her way through it until she didn't have any more tears left. She got dressed and made her way downstairs. She stood just outside the kitchen out of sight from the group. She listened to them arguing with Nate about her music because he was playing one of her playlists. It was the most ridiculous argument she'd heard in a while, but it was perfect. To understand how far things had come, they were family. Nate was family. Her dad accepted him, and that thought warmed her heart.

"My taste in music is awesome. It's you guys that suck," she said as she walked into the kitchen.

"There she is." Amir smiled.

"Hey, babe." She walked right to Nate, and he wrapped his arms around her and held her tight.

She pulled away from him and kissed him. Feeling his arms around her was just what she needed.

"Thanks, guys, for coming over. I know everyone is worried. I think my body just went into shock or something."

"Mir, where's Cheryl and the kids?"

"She sent me over to check on you. She's still not in a good way, and she didn't think she would be helpful. She sends her love."

"How are you holding up?"

"Doing the best I can," he said. "It comes in waves, you know? One minute I'm completely broken, and the next I'm laughing at something ridiculous he said. I know he would tell me to come and check on you, so here I am."

She hugged her brother tight.

They went into the living room and listened to a playlist of her dad's favorite songs she made for him. The sounds of Stevie, Charlie Parker, Fleetwood Mac, and Isaac Hayes filled the room.

"I see where you get it from," Nate said as he kissed her

cheek, and she snuggled up to him on the couch.

Cheryl eventually came over with the kids. Which was good for David, and he hung out with them. Amina smiled as she took in the room. Yes, this was awful. They all spoke of her dad in the past tense, and it broke her heart. They listened to all of the stories about her dad, told his bad jokes, heard his music through the tears. This was what he would've wanted, all of them together, enjoying each other.

She'd found joy. Amina wasn't sure how she would be able to hold on to it through all of this sadness, but she promised she would.

Mr. Michael Wright was laid to rest that Saturday.

Chapter Twenty-Four

"HOW'S IT GOING, bro?" Chris asked Nate when he went out for drinks with his friends after the gym. He needed a break. It had been about a month and a half since her father passed away, and Amina's grief was mind-boggling. He could never say or do the right thing, no matter how hard he tried. He wanted to be by her side through all of her grief, but it became harder and harder. He never knew which Amina he dealt with from minute to minute.

"It's been a rough few weeks. Amina's been all over the place with her emotions. She started seeing her therapist immediately after her dad died, which was great. I was proud of her that she knew she was going to need that help, you know? It's just been tough. She's having some of her girl-friends over tonight, which I was happy to see. She'd been so isolated from everyone except her therapist and me, so I was happy to hear that she was opening up a little bit."

"Oh, that's good," Shawn said.

"It's hard," Chris chimed in. "When my mom died, I had to take a leave of absence from work for like six weeks. I just couldn't focus. I would start crying one minute and yelling at someone the next."

"Yeah, she's got that going on. Her dad told me to be patient with her, said she was going to need me. I promised and so that's what I'm doing. The shit is hard. It's nice to be out with you guys for a little bit."

"Hang in there, bro. She'll be glad you did."

"Is she working?" Shawn asked.

"Yeah. She's swamped with work. They start planning now for that gala where we met. She said it takes months of work to put that on."

"It's always a lit event too. So I appreciate the effort." Shawn laughed.

"She's home really late. She's hardly sleeping. It's just a stressful time. She did say that once all the groundwork is laid for everything, it's just signing forms and making sure people are where they're supposed to be the day of the event. So that should be winding down soon, which is helpful. I just don't know what more I can do."

"Just be there, Nate, that's all you can do," Chris said.

"So, you not getting none either." Shawn smiled.

"Such an asshole." Nate elbowed him and laughed. It felt like he hadn't laughed in ages. "To answer your question, no, it's been a while. Which you know I understand. I haven't felt right trying to push on her when she's dealing with so much. I just have to wait, and I have no problem waiting. She's the one."

"Did you go shopping yet?" Chris asked.

"Yeah. Angela went with me a while ago, she and David. She got her size for me, and David was really helpful. It was a good time. I hope she likes it. I called her brother to let him know, and he was thrilled. I talked to his wife and their kids, and everyone is excited."

"Do you know when yet?" Shawn asked.

"No clue. I want her whole, and she's not there yet, and I don't know when she will be, but if I have to wait forever, I will. She's worth it."

"Good luck, man. I know she'll come around."

AMINA SIMPLY WASN'T in the mood to cook after the week she'd had. "Thanks for suggesting heading out for dinner tonight, Nate," she said, holding his hand as they waited in the lobby for a table.

"No problem, I figured you could use a break from cooking, and my horrible attempts at it." He smiled.

She felt the stares all around them and actually overheard a Black man who looked about her age say, "I guess we're not good enough."

She winced, but then she felt Nate's hand grip around hers. By her side, through anything.

Amina stood and turned to face the man who insulted them. "Excuse me, what did you say?"

"Er, um, I just don't understand. You know, we're not

good enough for you?"

"Who's not good enough for me? You? You probably are not." She chuckled. "I mean, pretty sure you're not better than him." Amina pointed to Nate.

He glanced up at her, and she leaned over and kissed his lips.

She pulled away from him and smiled at the rude man. "Perhaps you should concern yourself with your date and worry less about who's on my arm."

Amina smiled at the woman beside him. She glanced around the small waiting room and made sure that anyone else who shared this guy's thoughts and opinions kept to themselves. She sat back down next to Nate and slid her hand into his. She was done being afraid and being made to feel like she was doing something wrong. Her dad accepted him and their relationship, nothing anyone could say was going to stand in her way any longer. She held tight to her father's words to find joy in every single part of every day. Enjoy and embrace every moment, and she was determined to do that with everything she did, especially with Nate.

THE SUN WOKE Nate on Saturday morning. He started to feel a bit better about things with Amina. He glanced over at her side of the bed, and she wasn't there. Music played, and he smelled the bacon in the air. He realized she was up early in the kitchen, making breakfast, something she hadn't done or felt like doing in weeks. He splashed some water on his face, brushed his teeth, and hurried downstairs.

He found her in her robe, smiling as she sang along to her whiny music her brother hated. Her locs were up in a bun, and she looked like herself. She looked beautiful.

She turned around and smiled when she saw him. "Hey, good morning."

"Hey." He walked over, hugged, and kissed her. "What time did you wake up?"

"About nine. Everything is just about ready."

She fixed the kitchen table for them to have breakfast, and he was happy she looked like the Amina that he met so many months ago. He sat down and stared at her.

How long would this last?

"Thanks for making breakfast. Everything looks great." He kissed her on the cheek.

"You're welcome."

They started to eat, quiet, while soft music played in the background.

"Nathan. I know these last few weeks I have been a zombie."

He stopped eating and gave her all the attention she needed.

"I know that I have been up, down, and all over the place. Crying, angry, laughing, off into space in some moments. I know I have been a nightmare to deal with, and I'm sorry for that."

"Baby, you don't need to apologize. You have been dealing with so much." He kissed her tear-stained cheek and held her hands.

"I don't know how I would have gotten through this without you, Nathan." Her voice shook. He moved to hug her, but she stopped him. "No, please let me finish. I need to get this out.

"This is really hard. It's the hardest thing I've ever gone through. Sure, I was seeing my therapist, and she gave me the help I needed, and it helped. But having you here, to hold me while I cried. Texting my brother to give him updates on how I was doing because I couldn't talk to him, and I didn't want him to worry. Letting Angie and David know how I was because I know they were worried—letting me cry myself to sleep and not asking me questions. Me snapping off at you for no reason at all, and you just took it. You took a lot of shit from me over the last few weeks, and you would always walk away. I have no idea where you went or if there are holes in the laundry room." She laughed, and so did he. "You always came back, to endure whatever hell of a mood I was in."

He squeezed her hand.

"Nathan, I—I—I love you. I knew it that first night you stayed over. I felt so safe and secure with you by my side, and I knew you would protect me. I was just so scared. I didn't know what to do with those feelings. Then that night we saw each other at the bar. We have energy between us, it's undeniable, you know? We are meant to be. It is overwhelming how much love I have for you. I tried to fight it, but it's undeniable. I know it even more now after everything we've gone through since my father died."

Amina wiped the single tear that fell down his cheek.

"Nate, thank you. Thank you for caring for me the way you do. For being here for me the way you are. I don't know what I did to deserve you. To lead you to me that night we met, but I'm glad you did. I love you. I love you so much."

He stared in her eyes and stroked her cheek. "Amina, I've been in love with you for so long. From the moment I first kissed you, and every day after. You are the love of my life. I can't imagine my life without you." He pulled her onto his lap and kissed her.

He pulled away and gazed in her eyes. "Is there anything going on today?"

"Nope, nothing planned."

"Dinner tonight?"

"I would love that." She kissed him, and held him close.

HE WAS WAITING downstairs when Amina came down in a black fitted dress, her hair down and her favorite pair of Adidas on her feet. It had been a while since they had gone out, and the weather was finally starting to get nice again. Nice enough for them to walk over to their favorite restaurant in the neighborhood.

"Damn," he said, when she joined him, a smile on her face.

"If this is the reaction, you can never complain about how long it takes for me to get ready."

He kissed her cheek and whispered in her ear, "You look incredible, Amina."

"Thanks, Nate." She blushed.

It had been months, and he still gave her butterflies when he whispered in her ear.

They walked hand in hand to dinner. All the clouds that circled them for months finally broke free. When they got to the restaurant, they talked to the owner briefly and found a table tucked away in the corner like they usually did. He ordered a bottle of wine—no one was driving, so they could indulge a bit. Maybe they'd have two tonight.

"So, I have some good news," she said to him. "Everything is done for the gala. I won't be working these crazy hours anymore. It will ramp up as it gets closer, but for the next few weeks, things will be more normal."

"That's awesome news. You've been working so crazy. Do you think you'll ever not host the gala?"

"One year, they wanted some new chick to do it, and it turned out to be a disaster." She laughed. "So, it's been me ever since. I don't mind it, though. I meet so many nice kids and families. The stress of organizing it is not a good time, but knowing the impact it can have on so many people's lives, it's why I do it. So, no, it'll probably be me for a while."

"Is it okay for me to be your date?" He grinned.

"Oh, for sure. The creeper will be there."

He laughed. She missed this, spending time and laughing with him. She loved looking at his smile, and she hadn't seen him do that in weeks. His hands moving around feverishly as he laughed with his entire body—she missed it all. She had been so consumed with sorrow. She didn't think she would ever get back to these moments with him.

They ordered another bottle of wine and leaned a little closer together. Nate caught Amina up on all of Shawn's mishaps and shenanigans with his many women.

"One day, that man is either going to be on *Maury* or be on an episode of *Snapped*."

He laughed.

"I don't get it. He's not...well, he's capable of being a good, faithful man. Why does he choose to be this ladies' man?" she asked.

Amina had started to become quite fond of him.

"He likes being with different women all the time. When the right one comes along, he'll change, and it's going to be hilarious to watch."

"Are you ready to go?" Nate asked after a bit.

"Yeah, I'm ready to get home." She could not wait to be home with him.

"Good." He kissed her neck, and she shivered when she felt his beard against her skin.

They walked home as quickly as they could. When Nate opened the door, there were candles lit all over the house, with roses and rose petals adorning the staircase and leading to the living room.

Amina put her hands to her mouth, stunned. "How?" she asked.

"Had a lady on the inside." He winked at her.

"Wow. Nate, this is amazing. It's so pretty."

He held her hand, walked her over to the couch, and sat her down. Nate sat beside her and kissed her cheek while candles and bouquets of red roses surrounded them in the room.

She turned to face him, and he took her hands in his.

"Amina. I love you," he started.

"I—"

"Nope, I let you talk this morning. My turn."

She smiled at him.

"That night I went to the gala with Shawn, I planned on staying there for like an hour. Have a drink or two, watch him, and then at some point he would forget I was there and I would scoot out the door. I didn't want to go and couldn't wait to leave. Luckily, I saw you, and my life changed. I met the woman I was meant to spend the rest of my life with. I knew it the first night I kissed you right over there." He pointed to the foyer. "Every day since then, I've known. Even after you left that damn note.

"I know it's been a hard few weeks. Seeing you going

through all of this pain, knowing I couldn't do anything to take it from you, that was devastating for me. I felt helpless about the amount of suffering you were going through. I never want to see you hurting or sad."

A lesser man would've left.

"I made your dad a promise. He told me to be patient with you, and I promised I would. I promised I would care for you, keep you safe, and comfort you. So I did."

"You did." She wiped a tear from his eye.

He got up, kneeled in front of her, and pulled the ring box from his pocket. "The moment I kissed you, I fell in love with you. My love for you has grown each day ever since. You have made me a better man, a stronger man, a more understanding man, a more patient man. You are this beautiful, strong, smart, kind, giving, sexy, hilarious woman. You bring me so much joy and happiness; it's something I want to experience for the rest of my life. Amina Zahara Wright, will you please allow me to be your husband?"

Amina's smile was as wide as it had ever been. "Dr. Nathan Christopher Moore, I would be honored to be your wife. Yes!"

Nate gave a small fist pump and kissed her. He kissed her slowly at first, but Amina couldn't contain herself.

He pulled away from her. "Well, I have to put this on your hand."

She finally looked at the ring. "Damn, Nate." She couldn't believe her eyes. The ring was a princess cut, at least five and a half carats. She was speechless.

"I mean, you are marrying a doctor." He winked at her. "David helped pick it out."

"Wait. What?!" Amina yelled.

"Help on the inside, baby, help on the inside." He laughed.

He slid the ring on her finger. Perfect. She held it up.

"It's beautiful." She realized that music was playing, "Stronger than Pride," and she was reminded of their first night together at his loft.

"Over the last few weeks, I had some extra time. So I made a playlist for you."

He was a dream brought to life.

"That's very girlie of you, Nate." She laughed.

He took her hands, pulled her up, put his arms around her, and they danced as their song came on.

She used her fingers to trace the muscles on his arms. "Can we tell people tomorrow?" she asked.

"I'd prefer that."

She nestled her head against his chest and listened to the steady rhythm of his beating heart. She was entirely at peace. She turned and looked up at him.

He put his hand on her face, leaned down, and kissed her softly, taking his time. "I love you so much, babe."

"I love you too, Nate."

He put his hands up to the top of her dress and unzipped it. "I have wanted to get that off of you all night."

"Come here," she said and motioned with her finger.

He picked her up, carried her upstairs, and Nate was undressed in record time.

He laid her on the bed and was on top of her. "I missed you. I missed your body and how it feels."

"I know. I missed you too." Her heart raced in her chest as she waited in anticipation for him.

He kissed her from head to toe and she moaned at every touch. It felt so good to have his mouth on her. When he finally stopped teasing her, he let himself inside. She let out a small whimper of pleasure. Then he flipped over, putting her on top and holding her hips as she moved. He let go and put his hands on her breasts. Nate kissed them while she threaded her hands in his hair. He rolled her back over, and he put her arms above her head. He went as deep as he could go, then pushed still deeper. Amina had reached a height she never had. She lost all control.

When he came back to bed, he lay next to her. She sat up and looked down at him. "Nathan, please promise me that when we get married, this will never change." She laughed.

He laughed and wrapped his arms around her. "I promise as long as I am in working order, I will make love to you as often as I can."

She placed her head on his chest, where it belonged. "Nathan," she whispered. "Will you please move in with me?" Amina sat up, and looked in his eyes.

He kissed her and stroked his thumb across her cheek and her lips. "As soon as I can get the rest of my things."

Epilogue

"D ID YOU WANT me to meet you over there at this rate?" Nate asked as she finished up, getting ready for the gala. He paced their room at the Drake.

"Why are you rushing me?" She smiled. "I have to get up and speak in front of people, you know."

Nate needed to get out of this room as soon as possible. The longer Amina stood in front of him in that dress, the harder it became for him to keep his cool. She'd settled on a fitted peach strapless dress that made her skin glow.

She grabbed her purse, and they each gave a final look in the mirror next to each other and took a picture. "Perfection is what that is right there." She laughed as he leaned and whispered to her how much he loved her.

They walked out of the room just as Angela and her date walked out of theirs.

"Hey, guys."

"Hey, you two. This is a very different year, huh," Angela said.

"Yes, it is." Amina smiled at him.

When they arrived at the Field Museum, everything was perfect. The theme for the gala was a big top circus. Four aerialists were performing high above as they entered the main hall. The colors on all of the tables were reds, yellows, and blues. There were balloons all over the room, with small red and yellow couches spread out; it was a parade of vibrancy and fun, and every face had a smile on it. Everyone and everything was where they needed to be.

"Wow, Amina, this is amazing." Nate kissed her cheek. He was so proud of her.

"Thanks." She blushed.

"Where will I find you guys afterward?"

"I'll probably be at the bar. It's the clearest view to the stage." He winked, remembering that's where he first saw her this time last year.

"We'll probably be wandering around," Angela said.

"I'll just come to the bar, and we can all just meet back there."

"Sounds good. Good luck, babe. Be strong." He kissed her cheek.

FOR THE LAST few years, Amina always had a bit about her father in her welcome speech. This year she would be speaking about him in the past tense. The last thing she wanted was to turn into a puddle on stage for all the world to see.

The emcee got to the stage to kick things off. "Please welcome to the stage the lovely Amina Wright." *Here we go*, she whispered to herself. She got up there and spotted Nate pretty clearly. He waved at her, and she began her pitch.

"Before I go, I just want to leave you all with something, especially for the families who are struggling to deal with all of the health challenges for their little ones. Please hold on to the joy. Before my dad passed away"—*Hang in there, Amina*—"one of the last things he said to my brother and me was to find joy every day. And when you find it, hold on to it tight, and never let it go.

"When we were growing up, he told us we always see the big moments of joy and happiness, and we celebrate those and thrive on those. But it's the small moments that we miss. Those are the ones that keep us going, and those are the ones we need to cherish. So keep them close when they come up. Thank you to everyone who donates to our families. You are brave, and we support you. Have a great night, cut loose, and enjoy. Thank you."

She did it. The room stood up and clapped for her, to her surprise. The band played as she was on her way to the bar to have an incredible night with Nate. She was stopped a few times to shake some hands and take a few pictures with some moms and dads.

Then someone grabbed her arm. "You did amazing up there." Some random guy had come out of nowhere to put his hands on her.

She yanked her arm away and backed up. "Yeah, okay, thanks." She continued to walk away.

He stood in front of her and blocked her path. She was not in the mood for any of this bullshit tonight.

"What you said about that joy thing, it's so true." He stared at her like she was his next meal.

"Glad you got something out of that." She tried to move again, and he got in front of her. She sighed, annoyed.

"Can I get you a drink or something?"

"No. I think she's fine." She heard Nate's deep voice behind the creepy guy before she could answer. She smiled.

He walked over to her, grabbed her hand, and they walked away.

"So, next year, can you just meet me at the stage?" She laughed.

They went over to a small table, held hands, and stared into each other's eyes as if they were the only two in the room.

"You did really well up there. I know that was tough. I'm extremely proud of you."

"Thank you, Doctor." She leaned over to kiss him, and his hands brushed against her breasts. "Can we go now?" she asked.

"Are you sure?" He grinned at her in the way that set her on fire.

"Oh, I'm sure." She winked at him.

"I thought you'd never ask." He laughed.

She texted Angela.

They left the gala, holding hands just as they did last year, walking into a future, and life, together.

The End

Want more? Don't miss Shawn and Angela's story in *Maybe This Christmas*!

Join Tule Publishing's newsletter for more great reads and weekly deals!

If you enjoyed *There You Are,*
you'll love the next book in the…

Romancing the Doctors series

Book 1: *There You Are*

Book 2: *Maybe This Christmas*
Coming in October 2022

Available now at your favorite online retailer!

About the Author

Ieshia Wiedlin grew up in Detroit, Michigan, and currently resides in Brookfield, IL, which is a suburb of Chicago. She is married and has two great kids, Lucas and Zoey. She has always loved writing and telling stories, mostly sci-fi and fantasy, and is a huge junkie for all things Marvel and Star Wars. But somehow in the midst of loving all things sci-fi, she was a sucker for all things Molly Ringwald. Ieshia became a huge fan of rom-coms and loves stories with strong women characters. Growing up the youngest, and the only girl on her block, she craved strong women who fell in love. She loves romances with strong women leads who have conviction, but are also filled with humor. It's important to her that women in her stories are smart, strong, loving, and funny, and also represent for sci-fi geeks and music lovers everywhere.

Thank you for reading

There You Are

If you enjoyed this book, you can find more from all our great authors at TulePublishing.com, or from your favorite online retailer.

TULE
PUBLISHING

CPSIA information can be obtained
at www.ICGtesting.com
Printed in the USA
BVHW031712020222
627898BV00001B/60